Murtyl's Diaries: First Tears

by

Dr. Chris Pearson

Chapter 1: Introduction

1982: day of the meeting. Nick had been working for the Yorkshire Post since he was sixteen, starting as a deputy reporter in 1977. He was a smart young man who wore a shirt and tie, generally with a suit. His hair was clean and fashionably long, if not a little wild. His nose was of a size that if he wore glasses, they would not have fallen off. Full of fun, always joking and in the centre of the action, eyes glinting with a sparkle that the girls loved and the boys were wary of. He could be - and was - mischievous and a little rebellious. Although the editor didn't like it, he came to work in all weathers on his Kawasaki GPZ 550.

On this particular day he was called in by the editor. His heart sank; because of the strikes and the situation in the UK, he presumed either he was going to be sent on another information gathering assignment on Arthur Scargill, the miners or their strikes, or if it wasn't that, would he be thrown onto a three-day week or even worse, laid off like some of his colleagues? He made sure he was up and out of bed two hours earlier than usual to try and have some breakfast and get ready in plenty of time. Nick put a bowl on the table and went over to the cupboard for some cereal; he opened the cupboard door and then closed it again. Too worried to eat, Nick put the bowl away and decided he would go upstairs to get ready for his meeting with the boss.

He did his top button up, straightened his tie, pulled down the tails of his jacket, forgot about the oil under his fingernails and knocked on the editor's door.

Once the introductions were over, the editor smiled. He was a chap who knew what he wanted in life; his hair was perfectly combed back with dark frames around his glasses and he always had a clean-shaven face. Nick was congratulated on his diligent work and given his first personal one on one assignment: he was told to go to Hutton Rudby, about twenty five miles away down some challenging and fun twisting roads, the address Green View, East Side. The editor told him to speak to a friend called Murtyl. Murtyl now expected Nick to come for a chat and a bit of an interview. This, Nick thought, would be a bit of a challenge and a test on Sunday. Either way, he thought, as he walked out of the old man's office, he still had a job and this could be the start of more opportunities on the long road to becoming a fully-fledged reporter or writer, although there was always the possibility he could forget all this and become a professional motorcycle racer. This was his ultimate dream; he always dreamt about crossing the finishing line and everyone cheering for him. Nick daydreamed at his desk at work a lot; he always wondered about the outside world and what he could be doing if he was in a career with bikes instead of typewriters. But he never really thought he was good enough and anyway he didn't have the sort of money to be investing in such a career. Nick was the type of person who would try and help anyone out if they were in trouble, and he never seemed to stumble across any opportunities to make a profit himself.

Saturday was booked for practise at the local circuit, which distance wise was a toss-up between Oulton Park and Croft, the old aerodrome circuit near Teesside. Nick was looking forward to getting home that evening and doing his final preparations for Saturday's tests. Although his bike was second hand, it was new to him: a Yamaha TZ 250 G which had been purchased new by Armstrong Motorcycles. Their semi-professional rider, Alan Taylor, had won the British 250cc Championship five years earlier on it. All the tuning parts were still on it from that year; he had done well to get it out of Russ Amstrong, who owned Armstrong Motorcycles - a BMW and Honda dealership. Nick also knew that without the influence of Dave and Will Hardy of Saltwells

Garage, Middlesbrough, he would have stood no chance of getting his hands on the bike. Nick had to prepare the bike and his kit well and was hoping to set some good lap times on Saturday, to justify their help. This was the real dream opportunity - to have a go! Finances were a struggle but with the help and knowledge of Dave, Will and Webby, a previous Oliver's Mount Champion and Cock of the North, as was Dave Hardy, Nick knew he had the best people on his side; they were a formidable team.

Excited, Nick trotted out of the office but then realised this meant cancelling practice on Saturday as he would have to get some questions ready, and (miserably) no going to watch any racing on Sunday either. It also meant no tinkering with his bike or seeing his mates at his beloved sport of road racing. Going out for a beer on a Saturday night was now in the bin - he would need to be as fresh as possible to meet Murtyl on Sunday! With this realisation, his light steps through the offices became leaden and he started to drag his feet. Even though it was only 4.45pm on a Friday, he was about to leave work early to start his weekend. Nick had to acknowledge that being a top investigative reporter or writer was really his second choice of career. None the less he thought to himself, "Oh well, best get on with it!" He planned to go home and start preparing. He would then go out for a quick beer with his friends and tell them the news: he would not be out to play on Saturday. Nick planned to use Sunday evening to catch up with all the information on the lap times of his friends after his 'Murtyl' trip – he wasn't really sure what to expect but he was sure willing to give it a go, not just for his boss but for himself as well. Nick looked upon this experience as some sort of big adventure where he could just go out of the office and onto the open roads at his own leisure, gathering information - or at least that is what he thought it would be!

Sunday came; questions and notepads were

at the ready and Nick was all set to go. He had his best suit on with shirt and tie and his Barbour wax cottons over the top to make sure he stayed dry. All these items of clothing were very out of fashion and second hand, as were his boots, but Nick felt the part. Funds were scarce; he was only on twenty one pounds a week but he had managed to scrape enough money together to buy himself a new Arai helmet, which was his second pride and joy after the TZ Yamaha. Nick had to find money for lodgings, food and transport but to be brutally honest everything was second best to racing. The TV was rarely turned on, purely because he didn't have the time, but when he did turn it on, Nick just watched the racing or the results from the day before – even this gave him the ambition to do well. All he wanted was to cross the finish line first with the crowds watching – he could only imagine what standing on the podium was like as up to now he had never had the equipment to compete with the professionals.

Nick removed all locks and chains then checked the fuel and oil levels on the old Kawasaki GPZ. Once satisfied all was well and the drive chain lubed, he placed the key in the ignition, turned it, checked the choke was on then pushed the starter button. These Japanese bikes were good; she only ran one or two pistons up on the compression stroke before she burst into life. He sat for a few minutes, lightly revving her up and down from one thousand to three thousand rpm, warming her up slowly to reduce wear. The route he planned wasn't the most direct as he thought riding in straight lines was no fun, so he decided on a route that would allow maximum thrills and still be relatively quick. Nick was great at finding his way to places; he managed to navigate himself around the countryside as well the major towns and cities. He wasn't worried about travelling at all; in fact he saw it as an opportunity for plenty of speed and lots of cornering around the tight bends. This would scare some people but not Nick; he loved a challenge and if it was astride his bike – even better!

Nick set off on his journey. He came off the A19 heading North on the A172 past the Tontine Hotel, cloverleafed round over the A19 and then bore left down the A172. Nick really didn't like that smooth right-hander as it could suck you in - it allowed you to believe it was still a dual carriageway and to cut the corner. Davy Rudd, who was a friend of Nick's, was hit by a car doing just that and ended up in Friaridge Hospital, Northallerton for quite a while. This was not a thought Nick wanted to be remembering. He continued his journey, following the A172 for a mile or so, then took the Potto turn off to the left. Nick enjoyed the bends on the short road; going up and down the gearbox as appropriate for the corners, he kept an eye on the engine, making sure it was running at optimum rpm, optimising front-to-rear balance of the bike to get the best potential concerning speed. He loved to ride!

Oops! Foot peg and centre stand scraping the ground again, Nick smiled and made a mental note to remember to remove the centre stand and raise the foot pegs to allow greater ground clearance and angle of lean so he could corner at higher speeds. Nick came to the end of the short road and enthusiastically approached a T-junction, breaking down from ninety. As you can imagine this was fairly harsh using the gears under his left foot, throttle in his right hand and clutch in his left hand – altogether in perfect harmony. The road was clear.

After looking right and left a couple of times Nick then turned right, heading for Hutton Rudby, overtaking a few cars and smiling to himself. Nick started braking for the 30mph speed limit and glanced around at the properties to see if he could see where his appointment was. There was a church hall on the right, a little pub on the left and a little after that a funeral directors. Nick didn't think a pub and a funeral parlour so close to each other was the best omen.

Nick went over the little brow of a hill and he saw a really beautiful village green spreading out in front of him and another two pubs. Still unsure of where to go, he ventured left past the hair salon and the local Spar groceries shop. Further up that road there was another pub - The King's Head - a butcher's shop and a post office. Going down the green there were massive oak trees. Nick saw the names of the two pubs he had seen earlier: the Wheatsheaf was at the bottom and almost opposite was the Bay Horse. He parked outside the Bay Horse and stretched his legs before finding his destination. Walking out of the car park Nick crossed the road; he looked at the cottages next to the Wheatsheaf pub. Removing his jacket as he glanced around whilst trying to juggle his helmet off, he saw the cottage 'Green View' – bonus!

Nick sat outside the Wheatsheaf and finished taking his Barbour jacket off; he opened his rucksack, took his jacket out and brushed it down as well as checking his tie. He then knocked on Murtyl's door and waited a while but there was no answer, so he knocked even louder. Still no answer! This wasn't what Nick expected and he knew it wouldn't go down well with the old man, so he headed for the alleyway. Nick saw the kitchen door to the pub on his right and to the left of him was a Triumph TR6 650cc 1968 EBH 2 H. This was either restored or the owner was very careful. Nick checked the bike out: it had a two into one, up and over off-road style exhaust with Western bars on it. Wow, black and white in colour. Nick appreciated the classic and wondered what it would be like to ride the Triumph - not so easy, as the gear and brake levers on old British bikes were on opposite sides to the more modern Japanese style.

Back to business. He turned for the kitchen door of the pub and asked if anyone knew where he would find Murtyl.

Nick got his answers: "The other side of that bike, lad, in the garage; the bugger'll be there!" Thanking the man he wandered over in the direction he was advised and sure enough there was a pair of legs sticking out from under a car, with old brown overalls on - the kind used in the fifties and sixties by mechanics. The pair of legs was under a striking Austin Healey 100-6 in light Healey blue. The rear two wheels rested on a ramp and the front two were off, so the brake drums were exposed. Nick assumed the car was in for servicing but as he glanced around he then noticed the hydraulic lines were of braided hose, which usually meant the driver suffered from brake fade, raced or rallied the car – either way they probably drove rather enthusiastically. Nick was curious to know whether it had been tuned but decided it was time to crack on.

"Excuse me sir, I wouldn't suppose you could tell me where I would find a Mr. Murtyl?"

A sharp Yorkshire response swiftly came

back: "You'll find no Mister ruddy Murtyl here."

The pair of legs started to come from under the Healey. Then in one sweeping movement the torso came and slowly the head. Hands covered in black grease, a red bandana tied around the head, controlling long, black hair. Weird at first glance, and then Nick realised he was speaking to a blinking girl, or lady!

The lady stood up without saying another word, looked Nick up and down and then asked, "Biker, are you?" to which Nick replied,

"Yes ma'am."

She smiled quizzically.

Nick answered the lady. "Well yes, I suppose so. I'm trying my hand at road racing; ridden trials since I was thirteen and worked Saturdays for the Hardy Brothers down at Saltwells."

The lady smiled once more. "Know Will and Dave, do you? Must have a way to go mind, as they haven't mentioned no up 'n' coming Mick Grant!"

Nick was astonished; how did she know some people he knew, yet he knew nothing of her and had never seen her before? If nothing else he would have definitely remembered the Healey registration number: VAC736 and the bike as clean as it was in black and white. Nick doubted this was Murtyl.

She continued to speak: "You seem okay lad - Nick's your name, yes?" She held her oily, greasy hand out for Nick to shake.

"Yes ma'am but..."

The lady interrupted him. "Shake lad, never mind the muck. I'd be Murtyl, the one you're looking for."

Nick was amazed and wondered how she had come to know of him. Murtyl gestured for him to follow her towards the back door of the house, so off they went. Nick took note of Murtyl: she wasn't very tall - about five feet four inches. With the bandana on, it was hard to see but he thought she must have silky, dark hair and be approximately sixty years old or more. As she walked, her hips swung better than most girls he knew of his age.

Murtyl took her scruffy boots off as she entered the house and headed towards the kitchen. She washed her hands using good old Swarfega and then again in Fairy Liquid. Once satisfied her hands and nails were immaculate she pointed over to the tea bags and milk and said, "Get a cuppa made; there's some china cups there - use those and I'll see you in the dining room in a few minutes." Off Murtyl went leaving Nick to get on with making the tea.

On entering the dining room, Nick was fascinated with the photographs and trophies everywhere; this woman had obviously travelled around the world and he even recognised some of the race tracks in the UK in some of the photographs - Brands Hatch, Silverstone, Mallory Park to name a few - plus a boatload more that he didn't recognise. There were photographs of Murtyl with racing drivers and riders – she was a real looker in her day and boy she must have been around. Photographs included Stirling Moss, the great Argentinian driver Fangio – Nick had never seen such a collection! Mesmerised, Nick realised he was lucky to be sent here by his boss to interview someone who had lived his passion: fast engines, fast cars and fast bikes. He placed the cups of tea on the table and slowly looked up as Murtyl walked into the room. His jaw dropped! Not sure whether or not he had drooled, he thought he was dreaming - was this lady in her late thirties? She stood there smiling with long, flowing, slightly wavy dark hair just past her shoulders. She had a slightly long face, high cheek bones and strong eyebrows with crystal ocean-blue eyes you just wanted to swim in. Her nose was balanced with a few tiny little freckles and she had the most inviting red lips Nick had ever seen. Her broad shoulders were covered with a white blouse that was open at the neck, tapering down to a fine thin waist and then rounding out for her hips in a dark pencil skirt finishing just below her knees. Nick was glued; from the years on some of the photographs she must have at least been sixty.

Murtyl startled him and said, "I saw that twinkle in your eye and I thank you for that; glad I still have something going for me. I've spent a long time choosing someone to do this with, and everyone I've spoken to has mentioned you! They say you are someone I can trust, that you work hard and you're honest. Before I talk to you, you will have to win my trust and I can tell you, I know a bad one when I see one and I've dispatched a few in me time."

Nick's mind raced; Murtyl had obviously done her research and knew everything there was to know about him. What was all this about? How did she know all the people he knew and worked with? This was all getting a little strange. He stuttered, "Ma'am I only know how to be me; I make it my business to be the best of the best in everything I do."

Murtyl smiled. "I know you do Nick. I'm not accusing you, just stating fact. That is why I asked for you and only you! I've known Bill since I was a young one. He knows I've done some travelling in my time. He's seen the photographs! I promised him a few years ago if he found someone who was right for the job, I would reveal all – but only when the time was right." Nick was still overwhelmed and somewhat confused.

"Right, that'll do for now, get your gear on and enjoy yourself. You tell no one but Bill you were here lad - I'll be listening. If you do tell anyone, it's off, so keep your mouth shut and be back here three weeks next Friday, eleven hundred hours."

Nick just gazed at her. She raised her voice slightly. "Bugger off then, I've work to do on the old Healey!"

Nick tried to speak. "But ma… "

Again he was interrupted. "It's Murtyl lad, nothing else!" She smiled softly.

"Sorry Murtyl," he quickly corrected himself. "If you need a hand with the Healey I don't mind getting my hands dirty and what with the nights staying lighter for longer... " Nick paused and hoped she would say yes.

"Hmm, they said you'd volunteer - so be it!" Murtyl pointed to some overalls hung over her dining chair. "Put those overalls on lad, I'll go and change again, not be long."

Nick's grin couldn't get any wider across his face as he went over to the overalls and put them on as Murtyl had instructed.

Chapter 2: Gearbox, Dirt 'n' Grime plus a bit of Language

The prop shaft was off and the cables disconnected when Nick started to give Murtyl a hand. Together they removed the bellhousing bolts and all the other paraphernalia, then they gently levered the bellhousing back while taking the weight of the gearbox on a trolley jack. Nick didn't have a clue how they would get it from underneath the car but Murtyl had a plan and had obviously done this many times before.

"Okay lad, time for the lift!" She wandered over to the frame that was in the garage and lowered some clamps from the top which were attached to wires and, in turn, pulleys.

"Very clever!" Nick's face was a picture. "You're going to lift the gearbox up so the car can be wheeled out from underneath!"

Murtyl smiled. "Not just a pretty face am I lad?"

He continued to watch her and thought there was no wonder the Hardy brothers and the rest had taken to her – she was a genius, and beautiful! Nick wished he could speak of her to them, but he had vowed not to and a deal was a deal – no matter how frustrating it was.

The pair lifted the gearbox up over the 100-6 and again Nick was astounded. Pretty, intelligent and strong! He noticed the suspension was all uprated, the exhaust manifold was gas-flowed, there was a big sump guard and what looked like a super charger. Nick asked Murtyl about this and he just got a sharp response: "My old employer liked to know I could move if I needed to. Everything else will be explained if and when I choose to. Eye on the job now please."

Nick automatically replied, "Yes sir," and then realised yet again he had slipped up. "Sorry..." He tried to apologise but Murtyl interrupted him.

"Look it's either Chief or Murtyl, and

nothing else but I'd stress that you use Murtyl if you want to know what no one else does!"

Nick quickly answered, "Yes Murtyl, sorry." His lips were then tightly sealed.

They carried on working on the Healey; relined the clutch, changed the pressure plate and the thrust bearing, stripped the gearbox down and replaced the synchromesh on third. Nick was completely gobsmacked; he had never seen a group of men do this before let alone a woman on her own, but Murtyl took it all in her stride. She sat on a bench inside the garage taking things apart, cleaning them, checking the tolerances and then placing the individual parts in order.

"Why make it hard for yourself? This way, they are all clean and in the right order. A box of bits is hard to work with and takes up far too much time."

As Murtyl began to rebuild the box, each component was carefully oiled with Hypoid 80, otherwise known as gearbox oil, and checked to make sure the selectors moved properly. While doing this she also ensured the gears rotated and slid on their shafts. Nick sat quietly taking it all in; it was like watching a soldier strip and rebuild his weapon. Murtyl's rebuild was an inspiration; he was still convinced that she was too good to be true and that he had much, much more to learn - not just about her but the methodology and approach to the repair and building of motors.

Nick looked around the garage whilst Murtyl finished off what she was doing. He saw that everything had a place – some of her tools packed away neatly in toolboxes and others hung up on the wall in size order. There were buckets of screws, nuts and bolts amongst other things on shelves and she knew where to find anything she needed. Some of the garages Nick had seen were such a mess, the mechanics had to root through everything before finding one of their tools, but it was quite obvious that Murtyl had a very organised structure, and nothing was ever out of place – once used it was put back!

"Are you always like this Murtyl?" Nick wondered if it was just spotless because she had visitors or if it was like this all of the time. Murtyl didn't have a clue what he was mumbling on about.

"What do you mean? You could give me a clue at least!"

Nick laughed, "I was that enthralled I forgot! I mean, are you always so organised or is it because I am here that everything is neat and tidy?"

Murtyl looked up. "Less of the questions, but since you asked so nicely I suppose I will answer this once! I always make sure I put everything away, not just in the garage but in general too. You don't want everyone knowing your business, so in life, you must make sure that you put things back how they were. In my old job, it was a matter of life or death, so covering your tracks was really important and I never really got out of the habit of clearing up after myself, so to speak!"

Nick didn't have a clue what Murtyl meant but he smiled and nodded at her just the same. He was sure that he would find out soon but in the meantime he would just ponder.

Murtyl picked up her dirty cloths and made sure everything was away before she went over to the shutters. "Come on, enough work for today! Time to go home, the old lass will still be parked here in the morning." She smiled and waited for Nick to move so she could lock up; he dashed out of the way and they both walked over to the house together.

"Thanks for visiting, hope you have a safe journey home. Will I see you next week then?" Murtyl hoped she had not bored Nick. Although she had given him a few tellings-off, there was a likeability factor about Nick and she would love to spend some more time with him.

"I... if you will have me, Murtyl," Nick stuttered, hoping that he hadn't messed it up.

"'Course I will! Other than a few hiccups earlier, you have been a pleasure to be around! Enjoy your ride back home."

Murtyl waved Nick off. He shouted as he started to walk over the road for his bike, "Good bye and thanks again Murtyl, see you in a week or so. Take care!"

The engine was started up on Nick's bike and off he went down the road; he had the biggest grin on his face and was so happy. He had only known Murtyl for less than four hours and he already had visions in his head of some great times ahead! The roads were clear, so Nick got home fairly quickly. He took the same route back and went along all the bendy roads, cornering as hard as he could.

The boots he wore were pulled off and put on his doormat ready for work in the morning. Nick walked into the house with a spring in his step - he was so pleased to have met Murtyl and thought it was worth giving up his usual day's activity. It wasn't long before he was in bed. He sat up for ages thinking about what Murtyl had done that day and what she had said. In such a short time she had made an impact on him. He had never seen such activity being undertaken by men in such a small area, never mind by a single woman – if she could do this, what else was she capable of?

Chapter 3: The Deal

First day in the garage over with, Nick had learnt a lot about Murtyl already. Even though they had hardly spoken, he mainly just watched her and was fascinated with her work and attitude to life. She was logical and methodical in everything including her Healey and Triumph. Bill, the editor, just accepted the fact that Nick would now be with Murtyl every Friday afternoon. Nick became good friends with Murtyl; they started to get along and trust each other with their secrets. They spoke about braking techniques in cars and on bikes, how to use the faster line and where to find the grip and drive out of a corner. Nick was just amazed; he was happy and privileged to be in Murtyl's company – after all it was like she was a man in a woman's body - but she did sometimes speak, dress and think 'girly'. Murtyl knew her mind and what she wanted to achieve inside and out. Nick came to learn that she would have a drink with the lads, but it was always in her own style.

Fridays soon rolled around. Nick was so excited to see Murtyl - thoughts just bounced in his head from one week to the next. He was a very genuine gentleman; although he was young he understood trust and what he wanted in life. Murtyl enjoyed Nick's company; she grew fond of him and almost every week Nick went away with another one of her secrets.

"Many good old memories up here," she smiled, pointing to her head. "Full of adventures and past times. You remember: you keep them to yourself until I'm gone."

Nick nodded. "Anything you say Murtyl, you know you can trust me. I enjoy spending time with you and your Healey."

They pottered about in the garage, putting back the tools they had finished with as another Friday was coming to a close. The weather was really bad this week: it rained constantly and the clouds looked like they were full of the 'wet'.

"Would you like a cuppa before you go? See if this weather calms a little?" Murtyl waited for a response.

"Yes Murtyl that would be lovely, thank you." Nick was glad of the offer. “Don't thank me!" Murtyl said as she laughed. "You’re the one making the bugger." Nick loved Murtyl's sense of humour - she was very straightforward and just came straight out with what she thought; never held back. They pulled the shutter down on the garage and headed towards the kitchen.

"In you come lad, boots off – soap’s by the sink, you know the drill."

Murtyl did her usual - went upstairs and freshened herself up and changed into some clean clothes. She then paused, looking out of the window at the weather. "Anyway the weather don't look like it's settling - are you hungry? We worked well today - that Healey of mine is coming on well!"

Nick decided not to prey on Murtyl and her

routine; she obviously didn't want to speak about it if she were changing the subject.

"Yes Murtyl it's looking great, it won't be long before it's back on the road."

A couple of hours passed. Nick and Murtyl got carried away in conversation about the Healey and just general duties in the garage.

"You'll have to take her for a spin won't you? When she's ready." Murtyl smiled at him.

"Yes I'd love to!" Nick's face lit up. He was delighted and honoured that Murtyl trusted him with her baby, her pride and joy. "I promise I'll look after her."

Nick peered out of the window. "Ah the rain has stopped; better get myself home while it's dry." Murtyl seemed to be getting tired and Nick didn't want to overstay his welcome, so he went over to his boots and got ready to go home.

"You're welcome anytime. I enjoy you coming over; we'll talk some more about old times over a brew!"

Nick smiled. "Thanks, I enjoy being here, would love to hear about those times."

They said their goodbyes and Murtyl stood at the door to wave him off.

"Have a safe journey, won't you?" she shouted after him as he started his bike up. Nick rode off; he was really looking forward to hearing of Murtyl's past and having a drive of the Healey - he felt like he'd known her all his life.

The next day Nick got a phone call from Bill asking if he and Murtyl were getting on. Nick told him they worked well together and asked if it was possible to have some annual leave; Bill agreed. Nick wanted to surprise Murtyl and go and visit her before Friday; everything was packed into his rucksack along with a flask of tomato soup, which he had learnt was one of Murtyl's favourites, and a few bread rolls, freshly baked from the corner shop. Nick set off again on his normal route, which he was getting faster on, with Murtyl's advice.

He arrived outside. As usual the garage door

was open, two legs poking out from under the Healey. There were a few knocks from the engine bay before Murtyl realised she had company. "Hello - who's there? Can I help you?" she questioned.

"It's me Murtyl, I've taken some annual leave, and I thought I would come and take you up on driving the Healey - if the offer is still there and you don't mind of course!" replied Nick, going a bit red in the cheeks. He did get embarrassed easily as he was a sensitive young chap. Murtyl sped from underneath the Healey with a massive grin on her face.

"Lovely to see you again, long way off until Friday – 'course you will stay over; I'll put you up here!"

Nick was excited like a child at Christmas and answered straight back. "I brought a few things in the hope you'd say that. I also have some soup and fresh bread for lunch if that's okay with you?"

Murtyl replied, "That's fine with me, let's have an early lunch in a couple of hours then, and maybe we can strike her up later eh?" She smiled, knowing full well Nick would be up to the challenge.

"Yes! Definitely!" Nick almost jumped into his overalls. "What we on with today then Murtyl?" He brushed the Healey bonnet with his hand.

"Just a few bits, here and there - let's get stuck in and then we'll go for a spin after lunch," Murtyl replied.

They both got to work and managed to put it back together ready for take off; a couple of hours later they had finished – both looking a bit scruffy and their hands covered in oil.

"There you go lad," Murtyl threw the keys over to Nick. "Get your hands washed and then you can take me for a spin in the old lass!"

Nick caught the keys and dashed over to the sink to wash his hands as fast as he could; he was up for the challenge and wanted to hear some of

Murtyl's hints and tips whilst he was behind the wheel.

"Go for it!" Murtyl said, laughing, and followed him over to the sink to clean the oil and grime off her hands too. "Don't want to dirty my baby now do we?" They both laughed as they shared a towel to dry their hands and got changed.

All that was left to do was to start the old girl, run the pressures up and check all was shipshape.

"Want me to drive first, then you can take over?" Murtyl asked. She could see Nick was starting to look a bit nervous.

"Yes please," he answered – he wasn't nervous about driving at all usually but he felt a little under pressure because he didn't want to mess up in front of Murtyl or cause any damage getting out of the yard! Murtyl got into the Healey and turned the key to the ignition-on position. The Lucas fuel pump tapped away while charging the float bowls of the twin SU carburettors. She pumped the throttle twice just to get a little fuel through, then lent over to her left and pulled out the choke. Murtyl pushed the starter button; the starter engaged and cranked the straight-six 2.635-litre motor over lazily. When the second or third cylinder came up on compression she struck and ran up to fifteen hundred rpm immediately. Murtyl pushed the choke home a little to bring the revs down to maybe eleven hundred rpm, then checked the oil pressure was at sixty psi. She said it would drop to forty once the engine and oil were up to operational temperatures. The motor idled sweetly for ten or so minutes before Murtyl started to blip the throttle a little. What a heavenly throaty musical sound - the exhaust was like listening to a symphony.

Once the water temperature was up to eighty and no leaks could be detected, she beckoned Nick over. "Better get out for a run and get back to book her in for an MOT."

Nick wasted no time and jumped in straight

away. She spun the big Healey round, out of the courtyard and into the main street. They were off, and to Nick's amazement the old Healey pulled like a train. He could hear the whistle of the supercharger and was thinking, “This thing must produce some serious horses,” when Murtyl swung her into a series of bends. Murtyl turned her head towards Nick and winked at him. She faced forwards and dropped a gear and Nick’s heart jumped into his mouth; he grabbed the rail in front of his left hand. Murtyl calmly turned the steering wheel towards the corner a little early for Nick's liking! She then accelerated hard and the old Healey seemed to raise herself off the ground and go; the tyres stopped complaining and almost started to glide over the tarmac. By this time, Murtyl was into a four-wheel drift in perfect control and started to steer into opposite lock, which guided her beautifully towards the corner exit. The lock slowly came off and as the wheels stopped spinning she just accelerated away and then up into fourth, then overdrive. Nick was grinning like a Cheshire cat. Still stunned, he turned his head to look at Murtyl – she was cool, calm and relaxed!

She glanced back and said to Nick, "Hope you have some soup and a bun in the back somewhere, enjoying myself always makes me feel hungry. To Chop Gate then on to Helmsley for that soup."

Nick did his best to answer back but with the booming tone of the exhaust, the sucking draft of the twin SUs and the whine of the charger he gave up and just pointed forward as if to say GO! It was only when they caught up with some traffic that Nick got a chance to ask, "Did you ever take a driving test? Because they sure as hell don't do any of this fancy driving outside of the police and race tracks."

Murtyl just winked at him and said, "Yheeessss, something like that! I'm not ready yet, but I'll talk to you in time, that decision has been made!"

Nick was not exactly sure what Murtyl meant by that as she spoke in riddles most of the time, especially when her past was brought up in conversation. He sat in the car as low as he could, holding on to the grab rail. Murtyl and the Healey just didn't let off - swiftly up and down the box where appropriate to keep the engine spinning at its optimum. Sliding and drifting like he'd never seen before but always safe over blind crests. She overtook everything: modern cars, young lads in dads' cars, everything! Nick just wondered why and how she learnt to drive like she did - she was a very skilled driver and he knew this, just from one journey. There was something big Murtyl wasn't letting on, but he was sure he would find out in due course. His mind boggled.

They pulled up and ate the bread roll and soup, then went for a stroll around Helmsley. Murtyl looked over at a few parked bikes and told Nick about the pros and cons of two and four strokes. They laughed about the great smell of

Castrol R (a derivative of castor oil produced by Castrol as a four-stroke and two-stroke engine lubricant; their products were involved in a lot of the world's firsts for all forms of motoring).

"You know, if anybody ever can, I'll bet you a penny to a pound that if the odour was put into creams, soaps, shampoo, some bruising ointments and strain gear it would sell a treat." Murtyl had obviously thought about this beforehand.

Nick laughed. "Murtyl you're mad, what woman is ever going to go for a man who stinks of hot, burnt engine oil, adrenalin and a little sweat?"

She answered his question. "I did - the only man I ever loved, a French man, based at Elvington. He was a pilot, flying Halifaxes out on one too many missions over Europe during the Second World War. Sadly I never met a man who could live up to him. It got to a point where I stopped looking and focused on being the best of the best as you try to be!"

Nick thought this was a good opportunity to

ask some more questions. "At what, though, Murtyl?" Sure enough she answered his question but the answer was not what he thought it would be.

"I worked for the government directly and indirectly on a covert basis from 1943 until recently. I then retired and have put some facts onto paper, which can only go to the person I can trust to do the right thing. You will have to look at these facts and they can only be published once the statutes are out on the Official Secrets Acts I signed many years ago. I speak fluent French, Swiss, German and a little Arabic. I will tell you more over the next six to nine months before I leave. Then if you feel it would be of interest to anyone, you can tell my story, as it would be wrong for me to do so. I have given dates, times, places and some names, my personal parts and actions. From there, to an extent, you will have to research a few things to fill in some of the spaces I have left out - those things that were not a concern of mine. I trust you are beginning to understand what this is all about. In the meantime I expect to have some fun with you; I will help with your racing and we can do a little travelling." She paused. "Anyway enough of that, you going to drive us home?"

Nick jumped at the chance. "I'd love to, but not with the same kind of enthusiasm you drove here with! I don't know how you did that, it was bloody quick you know!"

Nick sat in the driver's seat and turned the key for the ignition and pushed the button to start the engine. He glanced over at Murtyl and said, "You can trust me with your life, you know that?"

Murtyl burst out laughing. "I already am," she said, stroking the Healey. "My life is much simpler these days than what it was."

Nick continued to drive them back but listened intently to every word that came from Murtyl's rosy lips. "When I was a young" she said, "my mother passed away, so I moved to Hutton Rudby."

Murtyl continued her stories from when she was a young girl, telling Nick of all the little adventures she got up to with all her friends. Nick soon pulled back into the garage and turned off the engine.

"Thanks for that Nick, hope I haven't bored you to death with my younger years," she joked.

"You never bore me Murtyl, I could listen to you all day," Nick replied and he was amazed.

"The good old days, people say," Murtyl continued. "I don't remember them!"

She never spoke of her jobs really other than working with vehicles and Nick wondered if she had ever had any other type of job, so he plucked up the courage to ask her. "Have you ever done anything else apart from work with machines, Murtyl?"

She looked over at him and smiled. "I became a kind of Civil Servant I suppose!"

Murtyl looked over at Nick. "Now get yourself off; I need a little rest, not had fun like that for a while! And when you're out on your bike at the track next I wouldn't mind seeing how you're getting on. See you later!"

Nick said his goodbyes and set off home with a great grin on his face. As he rode down the road towards home he thought to himself, "I really still have no bloody idea about the five golden rules where Murtyl is concerned. I really must remember to ask Who, What, Where, When and Why next time!"

Nick walked through the office doors bright and early on Monday morning only to find his boss, Bill, sitting on the edge of his desk.

"Have you got anything for me then? You have been visiting Murtyl for some time now and I am still none the wiser."

Nick replied, "No sorry, I know nothing, had lots of fun though!" He smiled, thinking about the drive the pair had yesterday.

"I am not sending you there to have fun, I have sent you there to do a job," Bill sighed. "I'm not having it, I am paying you good money for this and you have nothing at all?"

Nick repeated himself again. "No, like I said, I have nothing."

By this point Bill looked very annoyed. "Well I'm taking you off the case; I was obviously wrong about you, thought you would have done your job!"

Nick stood his ground, something he would not have done before he met Murtyl. "Well that is your point of view. I am doing my job if you must know, but if you are not willing to wait then so be it!"

Bill walked out of the office, muttering away. "Don't bother any more boy, I will find someone else." He slammed the office door shut behind him, leaving Nick in Bill's office. Nick thought to himself, if only he knew what kind of story there might be hidden with Murtyl. He must be under a little pressure.

After work Nick thought he had better pay

Murtyl a visit and let her know what the Editor had done and to let her know he was thinking about sending someone else out to interview her.

Murtyl didn't look shocked and just brushed it off. "That's fine and I'm pleased - this way there is no pressure on you or me. I have so much to tell you! I can only go so far; I will be long gone by then."

Nick, as ever, was quick to question. "But why?"

Murtyl sat in her armchair. "Sit down. I was young once like you are now." She continued, "My partner Albert Noir – Berty - and I have done a few odd jobs in our time - some above and some below the water line so to speak… "

Nick, like a schoolboy, stuck his hand up to ask a question. "But you never told me you had a partner!" he blurted out.

Murtyl burst out laughing. "No I didn't, and I haven't told you half of what I know yet - it wasn't that we were married or anything like that. If circumstances had been different maybe we would have been, but I can tell you the world would not be as it is today if that had been the case!"

Murtyl continued talking for some time and Nick sat there listening to her every word. "Tell you what, I'm going to rattle through a few years of my life and then slow it down. Don't take notes, just use your memory - I know how retentive it is. You promise me that when the time is right you will get this stuff out?"

Nick wasted no time replying, "Certainly Murtyl, I promise."

Murtyl sighed with relief. "I wouldn't like to think the few months I have known you had been wasted; what Berty, my team and I have done over the last forty years should become public knowledge."

Nick swallowed hard and wondered what the bloody hell she could be on about! "Murtyl you're a nut in a car, what on earth have you done and what's this about 'my team'?" He didn't think that Murtyl would be telling him all this today, but he was always happy and ready to listen to everything she said. Murtyl had so much knowledge and experience in life that he seemed to trust and believe her every word.

Murtyl spoke in a soft, soothing tone. “At the beginning, always start there, just like stripping an engine! Step by step, keep it as simple as one, two, three. Just don’t let me down,” she reminded him again.

Nick understood she meant business and thought he ought to tell Murtyl what he thought. “No Murtyl I couldn’t do that, my world has changed since I met you! For some reason my focus on the track is better and I listen more intently, as you have pointed out so many times before.”

Murtyl just replied, “Listen twice as much as you talk, be aware of being aware, and if you only think you know - then you don’t, so shut the hell up!”

Nick nodded; he knew she would have a

sharp, sarcastic response ready and waiting for him if he spoke now!

Murtyl then changed the bloody subject and said, "Right, are we going for that drive? It will give my mind a chance to get everything in the correct order for you." She smiled and looked in the direction of her bike gear.

"Sure Murtyl, I'll get ready right away," Nick added.

They rode out together, out of Hutton Rudby past Stokesly and headed via the back roads over to Danby on the North Yorkshire Moors. Murtyl took the lead quite slowly at first, making sure her position was correct and Nick had plenty of time to get through junctions with on-coming traffic. Her Triumph burbled beautifully! Once away from built-up areas, she started to pick up the pace a little and seemed to relax while he dutifully followed her, on roads unknown to him. She picked up the pace again once she was comfortable on her Dunlops. Even with the twin-leading-shoe front drum brake, Nick was learning she had no disadvantage in deceleration against his twin discs. Odd puffs of blue smoke popped out of her exhaust on the overrun and when changing up a gear. He was getting the smell in his head now and beginning to understand her statement in Helmsley a few weeks ago.

She started to tip her Triumph into a few bends even more enthusiastically now and Nick was beginning to wonder if he could keep up. What with the gravel here and there and damp patches, it was getting a little hairy, yet Murtyl just took it in her stride, as if it was perfectly normal to be going at that pace. Coming over the two humpback railway bridges and a few sharp rises she either had the front or both ruddy wheels off the ground! That TR6 seemed to rev high too, not the expected deep thrum from the standard long-stroke, parallel twin but a thrapping sound that was like thunder out of that Siamese two into one up and over exhaust. She got the odd slide on, mid-corner; her inside leg would hover off the foot peg and drop a little, then she'd drift the Triumph out under power. It was almost like being at an exhibition. Nick really did have so much to learn from her! Then just as calmly she pulled up after going through Danby and placed her bike just round the back of a farmer's gate out of sight. Nick followed suit.

The view was magnificent! Murtyl took him for a walk towards the river Esk which would eventually escape into the North Sea, through the centre of Whitby. There were butterflies all over the meadows, curlews singing their amazing songs in the fields and the smell of the freshly cut hay was fantastic.

As they got closer to the river, Murtyl started to roll up her sleeves, then bent down and took off her boots. Then as she walked on she took her pants off, leaving them behind her in the grass. Nick was beginning to panic; what on earth could she be expecting from him? While doing this she asked Nick to keep his head down and keep quiet. As ever, he was confused and tried to work out what she was up to!

Murtyl moved a little further up stream to a banked shallow area with quality flowing water, just above the entry to a pool. She stepped down into the weeds; he started to relax as she slowly walked upstream through the weeds. Carefully she pushed her hands into the weeds; they would occasionally come up out of the water. Each time she would rub them together slowly, then she would start again. Neither of them said a word, then she started to smile and slowly looked up at Nick and winked with one eye.

All of a sudden Murtyl hauled herself up, straightening her back, letting her arms smoothly and quickly come up out of the water, as she shouted, "Dinner!" and a great two and a half pound brown trout flew over towards Nick a few yards back. Nick looked at her in astonishment; he had heard of those who could tickle trout but had never seen it done before. Murtyl quickly came over and dispatched the trout, smiling at Nick. She eased a few quiet words out to him. "I'll explain over dinner lad!" She giggled at him, his jaw wide open as if some sort of miracle had happened. Then she found her pants, pulled them on, and got the rest of her gear sorted ready for the ride home. Then, they were off.

Once they arrived, the trout was gutted and Murtyl cooked it over a barbecue after drying it slowly, packing it with butter and parsley, then drizzling lemon juice over it. There were new potatoes on the boil, and some French beans to go with it.

Together they sat down to eat. Nick just ate and waited for Murtyl to start to talk. He now knew, as she had explained, that he had been 'born with two ears and one mouth' and he should use them in that order. He also knew that whatever she was going to say would have a profound impact on the rest of his life. Then she began:

"I grew up here in this village a few generations ago… most of the people I knew, left during the war – and sadly not that many were to return. My best friend was little Cerian; she was beautiful, such a pleasant girl to be around."

Murtyl smiled. "She was always laughing, joking and smiling about everything. We liked to play tricks on each other too, in between doing all sorts of other things! She was the only girl I used to play with - all my other friends were boys. Cerian was so quick-minded and sarcastic; sometimes without knowing I think, she used have us all laughing at school and out on the green. I'd be five years old, maybe six then. Life was just fun; we fought with other gangs, stole apples and if there was trouble to be had - we were always first to find it!

'Cerian was blue-eyed, with long blond hair and a smile that I'm sure later in life was going to melt a few hearts. She had the quickest wit and mind I have ever come across. She would have me in stitches with her cheek."

Murtyl carried on for some time and Nick quite happily sat there and took it all in. "I have some old prints somewhere of us all when we were younger lad, would you like to see them?" she asked.

Nick didn't quite know what to expect but he loved hearing of Murtyl's past so he agreed. "Would love to, Murtyl."

She reached behind the sofa and pulled out a tattered bag; it looked years old and had plenty of rips and tears in it. Nick leaned over towards Murtyl and wondered what it was he was going to see and whether her life had always been so hectic.

Chapter 4: Early Years and Tomboy Fun

Murtyl made a pot of tea and brought it to the dining table where she spread out some of the albums. She was grinning at some of the photographs as she opened the first album. "I was such a tomboy when I was younger, you know," she laughed. Nick asked why this was.

"I was more interested in building things and making carts to go downhill racing!"

They had finished flicking through the first album. Murtyl picked the next album up, this one covered in dust. "Have a look at some of these!" She passed Nick the album; there were all kinds of photographs - of course they were black and white prints but you could still see what was going on in them; others were hard to make out but Nick managed to use his imagination to piece them together.

"Looks like you had lots of fun in these photographs Murtyl!" Nick was amazed. "You must have lots of memories."

Murtyl laughed. "That's just a few." She paused.

"But these here, I mean look at that!" He pointed to something that looked like a go-kart. "Did you build that?"

Murtyl peered over at the photograph Nick was looking at. "Yhheeees, well, that was the day the boys, Cerian and I decided that we would build our own and then race them down the big hill past the green! I beat them all that day - one of my first ever wins." She grinned.

"You give the impression... " he paused.

"Go on lad, spit it out!" Murtyl started to grin, wondering what he would come out with this time.

"Well, you give me the impression that you are very strong-minded and you don't seem to let life get you down!" Nick looked over at her from his chair and smiled.

"Life is too short; you have to live it while

you're here because you don't know what's around the corner. You just got to get on with it! You will stay tonight? There is a spare room if you like. I would be grateful of the company."

Nick agreed to stay; she made them both a cup of fresh tea and they sat in the room with the fire on and got the map out. Murtyl pointed different routes out and explained where they led to, why she went on them and where she ended up on them.

"I know you are wondering why I know all this stuff lad. My father was a busy man travelling Europe, and he had survived the First World War in the military and was very well to do, so to speak. He then became a negotiator for the British Government in the sales of arms. Hence he travelled and attended conferences throughout Europe and Africa, taking me with him in the summer. He taught me to shoot small arms from the age of twelve, to tickle fish, snare game and how to survive as well as defend myself. He seemed to know that the Second World War would happen and was trying to protect me, or at least give me a fighting chance if the UK was ever invaded. I could, in my day, shoot the ace out of a playing card at two hundred and fifty yards with no eye assistance. Not too shabby!"

Murtyl continued. “So when I was in the Hutton Rudby area and not at school, living with my father’s mother, my gran, I would get up to mischief with Cerian all over the place, poaching and doing boys’ things better than the boys. A gamekeeper did catch us once or twice but once he got to know us, he taught us a few things. Yes, good old Kev Mooney - now he was a good one, with horses too! That's how he caught us the first time. We thought we had the measure of him, but didn’t think he could do several five-barred gates and a few hawthorn hedges as quickly as he could, and get back round in front of us. He took us to my Gran's where I got a good tanning from her once she knew we'd been caught.

'As time went on Kev started to look after us a bit and taught us a lot about tracking, survival and how not to get caught. He was always full of fun and used to get us to place bets on the point-to-point races he competed in. I'm pretty sure he must have been a damned good jockey and supplemented his income that way, as I never saw him sell any game on the side to the local butcher. Maybe that's the meat we got to take home, who knows! Kev was about five foot four, tan-coloured hair with a side parting. Bright, bright blue eyes and sharp as they come. Quietly spoken, kind and patient, but he never missed a thing.

'Once, we borrowed a few snares and traps when he was away for a couple of nights with his wife. We put them back, clean as you like and not a thing out of place. The bugger still had us up for it; he was just one of those people with an eye for detail. We quickly learnt that no matter what you're up to, miss the detail and go for the big picture! The job will bite back, no matter what you're up to," Murtyl laughed.

Chapter 5: Travelling and Meeting Berty

"Anyway I've digressed. Once I got a bit older and was pushed at school, the only things I had trouble with were languages. So my father would take me on his trips abroad in the summer holidays. He seemed to know everybody of importance wherever he went. We would go to car races all over France and I was introduced to Willy Grover-Williams and his wife Yvonne, and Robert Benoist - two great Grand Prix drivers based in Paris. Then there was Jean-Pierre Wimille and his wife to be, 'Cric'. I was often left with them and their families when Dad had special meetings to go to. They were great days in 1933 to '38. I was in and out of Bugatti dealerships and taken all over by them. They even taught me to drive in a 1932 Austin 7 and I competed in hill climbs and races - Robert and Willy bought her for me! You haven't seen her yet Nick, she's beautiful: gunmetal grey over old English white and still ready to race! I keep her just up the road in Gary's garage. I'll take you up and show her to you soon, maybe even go out for a spin!

'Robert was a World War One flying ace too; once I found out I pushed and pushed to get a ride in the air. He did eventually take me up and try as he might he couldn't make me ill. So the next time he started to teach me to fly; it was great fun and held me in good stead for the ATA not that many years later. I think I had my Wings before I ever drove a car on the left hand side of the road."

Nick interrupted her. "I think I can see where all those pictures came from in your house. I've never heard of those three guys before though; why is that?"

Murtyl continued: "Well," she answered, "there is no denying they were the best in their day and sadly for us they never got the chance to really show how good they were against Fangio and the like. The Nazis SS made sure with their 'special treatment' that they never got to the last day of the war, although the French did not forget them and even held a race through the streets of Paris, on what turned out to be VJ Day, in honour of Benoist. There were a few of us cheering the cars on that day - possibly as many a one hundred thousand people. They had set the track out through the centre of Paris to give the best access for all… it still makes my heart ache to think what they endured."

Murtyl just seemed to want to talk. "When I was twelve or thirteen, and Father went to Spain or Africa, I would stay with the Noirs in Marseilles in France; they were at a diplomatic level. I got on with their son Albert. The other kids used to torture the two of us as posh kids. It didn't take too long to find out after a few tight squeezes that we seemed to work well together. He would know what I was thinking and I would know when he was in a tight corner. He was good with his hands and I was getting better all the time. He even showed me how to use a sling and a bowline once he knew

I could hunt. I was able to show him a few of the tricks Cerian and I had learnt from Kevin and these things seemed to cement a lifelong friendship.

'Sadly for me, everything came to an end when the political tension in Europe became too great. Chamberlain said there would be peace in our time. As we all know there had been several years of unbelievable nastiness in Germany as Hitler and the Nazis took over and built their war machine. They came out to motor races with unbelievable government financed A.U.s and Mercedes racing specials which Willy fought against in the 1929 first ever Monaco Grand Prix. He was stuck in top gear for the last few laps, yet still brought his Bugatti home the winner.

'Once the invasion of Poland started in 1939, nearly all us Brits flooded back to the UK to do whatever we could in the war effort. Sadly I rapidly lost contact with Albert, Jean-Pierre, Robert and Willy's families; I had to focus on doing what I could. So I started as a land girl; worked my heart out, but once they realised I was pretty handy with engines and could drive, I was brought into driving ambulances and so on. As it came out in discussions that I had flown, I was swiftly recruited into the Air Transport Auxiliary and ended up flying all forms of aircraft from manufacturers, once they'd been trimmed, to the operational bases all over the UK. We were never armed and once or twice I was attacked by ME109s while trying to get aircraft to places such as Biggin Hill and Manton. I managed to elude the Messerschmitts using the skills I gratefully learnt from Robert. It was hard work getting into a new aircraft, anything from a single to a four-engine beast; working off a one-page notepad with start up, take off, cruise and landing procedures.

'Once you landed safely at the destination you were quick smart turfed out; the idea was to get any form of transport available to get back to another manufacturer, and take another new aircraft to its assigned squadron. I loved it. The pressure was great, of course - there were days with the old taildragging aircraft, where the wind speed was too high at the take off point or destination; then we were grounded and not allowed to fly. We had to spend time entertaining ourselves. Whenever it was possible I personally went out to poach whatever I could, as I was always so damned hungry on those ruddy rations. It always seemed to me wherever I did this that the civilians who built the aircraft or the crews on active bases were pretty pleased to have extra meat rations because I happened to be there. Nobody ever asked where I got it from, so I never let them know.

'One particular day I was delivering a Halifax four-engine bomber to Elvington operational airfield just outside of York. I came down and landed, thinking bloody marvellous - I might just get a couple of days at home as it's only twenty five miles from here. I could get the train from York to Thirsk, then get off at Yarm and walk from there.

'As it happened I taxied the aircraft in at around 1800 hours; shut her engines down, all mags off, fuel and electrical circuits and I alighted from the aircraft. While I was walking across the apron towards the control tower to get my logbook signed I nearly fell to my knees as my stomach churned and turned over. I didn't understand at first; as I turned and grimaced, I saw Albert Noirs heading out to an aircraft that was flying out on a mission that evening. I just prayed that he'd be coming back as I now realised I loved him."

Murtyl paused for a few seconds to catch her breath. "I went to see the Squadron Commander very briefly - knocked on his door. I knew this wasn't the done thing but I needed to confirm what I already knew. He answered my knock with the word 'enter' in the most unbelievably, highly educated kind of stuffy tone. The Wing Commander sat there, leant back in his chair with his tie done up tightly and his classic

Royal Air Force style moustaches, black hair crew cut with neatly trimmed short sideburns, sporting a bit of a tan as it was towards the end of spring. As he looked me up and down I noticed he was a bloody big feller, guessing he must be at least six foot two inches and a little portly. It seemed he had decided for himself that he was a cut above me but that didn't matter. I had to know - was that Albert?

'I said to him, "Excuse me Sir, I've just dropped off your aircraft and am leaving to go home. I know this is a French squadron and there is information you cannot give me but I think I saw an old family friend, Albert Noir; could it really be him?'

'The Commander replied in his deep baritone voice, "I cannot confirm nor deny that we have a wonderful pilot by that name," as he winked his left eye at me. My heart fluttered; I knew the bastard was here. The Commander then nonchalantly said, while stoking and lighting his pipe, pulling the flame deep into the tobacco, puffing plumes of fragrant blue-grey smoke - which stank…"

Murtyl winked at Nick and continued the story. "The Commander was tapping a rhythm with his left index finger on his desk. "If someone was to leave their contact details on a piece of paper, on my desk, and that person you asked about actually existed, it may just find its way to him." He smiled knowingly at me while pushing a pencil and piece of paper across his desk. I jotted my name and address on the paper and slid it back in the Wing Commander's direction. I spotted the nameplate on his desk and then told Wing Commander Jack Butler that I was much obliged. He nodded in acknowledgement, gestured with his hand for me to leave and quickly mumbled, "I've not seen you here" as I exited the office.

'Jack later became a lifelong friend and was often a go-between, for later operations with various sovereign states. His personal intermediary and liaison skills even saved my bacon a few times!

He was also damned good fun to be with when he was off duty!"

Murtyl carried on. "I went to leave the aerodrome, looking for anybody I could thumb a lift with from Elvington to York. It was evening, around seven o'clock; I got a lift to the city wall and briskly walked through the city centre. All the shops were closed. I glanced through a few windows but in my heart I was somewhere else completely. I kept my fingers crossed for Albert's safe return and that he would be given my note.

'At the railway station I bought a ticket from York to Thirsk, then on to Yarm. Boarded the train - amazingly enough, there were few people on the train. I sat and daydreamed, half-smiling to myself that Albert was possibly so close and would get in contact. I stared at the lady opposite doing her knitting; I reminisced about the adventures that Albert and I had in our younger days. As my mind focused more and more on remembering how we had got on, knowing what each other was thinking, supporting each other in our battles and fun times when I had been living with his family, I began to realise how much I had missed my contact with him since the war had started, and desperately needed to see him. I think that was when I realised that he would probably be one of very few, if not the only, person I really gave a damn about.

'I got off the train at Yarm and walked home - it was only six miles from the station to Hutton Rudby. I thought to myself, if Berty really was here, I wanted to save every penny I had, so if Berty did make contact we could at least do some special things together. Crazy things went through my head: I wondered if he had any leave to take and where could we get away? Would I be able to get some leave at the same time? If all went well would he come and live with us, when he was not operational? What was the future for us - would he be safe and get through the war? Would I for that matter? What did the future hold?

'So Nick, at that point I had a couple of days

off and spent them at home with my gran, fettling my father's motorbike, knowing this would be the best form of transport. I knew Berty was definitely in the UK but I didn't want to get my hopes up in case he never made contact.

'Over the next couple of days, two men in business suits and bowler hats, holding brollies, knocked on the door as they did every two months and asked was there a letter for them. There would usually be a letter from my father every two, three or four weeks to my gran and me, plus a third letter that would come alternately addressed to my gran and me - except this had a number '5' on it – this was for the men that came. The first one we ever received was a little note to us from my father, to say that any envelope which came from him with the number five in the address was not for us - these letters would be picked up by London businessmen. I believed they were actually intelligence people because one month a letter would be from Lisbon and a while later they would come from Switzerland. Six or nine months after that they would appear from Australia and I still don't really know what he did - not fully anyway! The gentlemen, before leaving, would always say, "Thank you ma'am. We would just like to let you know that the person you are interested in is safe."

'This went on throughout the war, until one day they came and did not say he was safe but had to regretfully inform us that the person we were interested in, being my father, would not be returning. Sadly I never found out what he did, how he did it, when he did it, or where he did what he did. Later when I left the ATA and joined the Special Operations Executive I found out that he was a highly respected man!"

Chapter 6: The Times, MI5 and SOE – Murtyl's Work Life

"Sorry this is taking a long time, this is not even half of it. Do you want me to continue?"

Nick answered straight away. "I would love nothing better Murtyl, I'm hooked!"

She took a sip of her tea and continued where she left off. "The day after that, I received a telegram which made my heart sing, because in those days, telegrams tended to be bad news. But it read: 'Gifted three day pass STOP HR tonight 1900 STOP Berty'.

I slapped my thigh with my hand, while having the biggest grin on my face and replied, 'Please reply "Merci" STOP'. I literally jumped for joy, ran back to the house, grabbed my gran and told her she would finally meet Berty, the boy I fell in love with! I squeezed her so tightly that day; I stood back and she saw the light in my eye. And then I was shaking – she could read me like a book, my gran.

'She glanced me up and down, winked at me and said, "If it's right lass, it's right." Then she told me to turn tail, get changed, get on to Kevin's beat and get something special for dinner. I came back three hours later with two brace of partridge. I was that excited - I made Kevin a few brews and told him all about Berty!" Murtyl laughed. "I can remember it like it was yesterday! Strange that the brain never shuts off, isn't it?"

Murtyl gave him no time to answer. Nick quickly nodded before she continued, "I was thirteen years old when I first met Berty - my father, as he had done before, had left me with a family I did not know. But rather than it being with Willy Williams, Robert Benoist or Jean-Pierre Wimille, this time it was with Berty's parents. Berty's father was the police commissioner for Marseilles and he oversaw the customs. Marseilles was a hard city as it had many, many nationalities there, being a seaport; strangers were continuously in and out.

At first when I stayed there it felt almost like a military camp, but once it was explained what his father did for a living, I began to understand the difficulties they had in life from various factions and people who were either smugglers, cut throats, vagabonds, thieves or spies. Berty and I would pretend that we were special agents after listening to plays on the wireless. We would re-enact the various plays that were broadcast - this involved hand-to-hand combat which we became quite skillful at, through the use of books, practice and occasionally his father would invite the head of combat training instruction for the police to afternoon tea. We would get him, whenever we could, to train and develop our knowledge and skills. We did this for the month that I got to spend with them every year; we seemed to develop an almost instinctive or telepathic ability to know what the other was thinking.

'When we left the grounds of his father's

property occasionally, we would be taunted by the local kids; they would attempt to guide us into an area where they could provoke a fight. The intention was really to nick some of our clothes and any money we may have had. The two times we were cornered, we fought our way out and left a right bloody mess behind us. Berty's father did take us to one side and explained to us how privileged we were in our upbringing, skill sets, speed of thought and reasoning. Later in life, if what he feared was to come about, we would be very glad of the tools we were learning. He slapped us both round the back of the head and said, "'But don't bloody well use them on my patch." He was so stern with us that day!"

Murtyl barely came up for air; she was definitely on a mission to reveal most of her life to Nick. "Bless my gran, she set off cooking the birds after I'd plucked and dressed them. I went upstairs, washed and put my Sunday best on. Painted the nylons lines down the back of me legs, as was done in those days because nobody could get hold of them except the Americans, who, to tell the truth were paid too well compared to us! Then I decided it was not me to be dressed up like a dog's dinner, so I washed my legs and got changed again, putting my slacks on and a blouse and then did the best I could with my hair.

'After that I set off for the bugger. It was around 1840hrs and was too late to go and pick him up, even if I had the fuel to put into Father's bike. So I dropped into the Wheatsheaf next door and told the landlady Jo who was coming. She had listened to my adventures with Berty since I was thirteen or fourteen years old, and was quite excited to meet him. Jo had been left the pub when her partner had been hit in Flanders during the First World War. She never talked about it. The village had lost quite a few men in those sad days. She gave me a drink of lemonade and listened to my excited drivel, which I know helped me relax. I think this was the first time I was ever nervous.

'Jo was really good to me and my gran. If there was any food left over from the pub when I was away, she made sure my gran got the lion's share, in exchange for a bit of cleaning, spud peeling and general help around the place. For me, it meant I knew someone was looking out for my wonderful gran while I was away working.

'After speaking to Jo for some time it was 1915hrs so I set off up the village, and dropped into the King's Head. As I said before I never took to drink but old Wrightson the landlord knew me well, as he liked his bikes too! If there was a chance we would ride out together over the moors and occasionally race each other on top of Carlton Bank, where we had a pretty rough but fun scrambles track laid out. A bit of elbowing and kicking used to go on - the trophies were pretty even over the years. He was trying to talk bikes and tell me about the recent raid on Teesport and the steel foundries but I just blurted on about Berty.

'Then I told him I had to leave sharpish and I

was off, not too sure how to meet or where to meet him. I ended up by the little memorial at the top of the village for the heroic men lost in the First World War, and sat just waiting to hear his footsteps. After ten minutes or so, my tummy started to churn and I felt a bit sick! I heard a faint whistle coming from along the road toward Craythorne; at first I didn't recognise the tune - then it dawned on me! It was the old French song his father used to play most evenings when I stayed in Marseilles."

Nick interjected, "And then what Murtyl?"

Murtyl carried on speaking. "Instinctively I got up and started to run towards the whistle; he must have seen me before I saw him, because he was running towards me too. As we got really close we both stopped and just looked each other up and down. He had grown into a really good-looking man and had definitely lost his boyishness. He let out the loudest wolf-whistle I had ever heard! He then put both arms out and I ran into them, kicking both legs up into the air and wrapping them around his waist. He spun around; I cried with joy and promptly began to look a real mess!

'He just kept saying, "I prayed you'd find me, ma chérie. Always together now, always! No matter the situation we work as one to love and protect each other." 'We kissed for the first time ever, then strode through the village hand in hand, to my home and Gran for dinner."

Murtyl yawned. "I'm getting tired you know lad, but there is so much I need to tell you about me and Berty!"

Nick's eyes were wide open. "I am all ears Murtyl." He smiled softly at her and waited for her to continue.

"Berty and I, we were one of a kind. We knew after the first kiss that we were meant to be; we ended up spending the next seventy two hours together. I showed him around the village and introduced him to all the people there – they loved his sense of humour and his loveable character! We went hunting together – caught all sorts of things in many different kinds of traps. I told him I had a good teacher! I introduced him to the gamekeeper, Kevin Mooney.

'The night I introduced Kev and Berty to each other I found out an answer I had wanted to know for so long: Kev told me the secret to his riding ability! I would have never have guessed in a million years - he used to ride King George the Fifth's steeplechase horses! He was one of the best jockeys back in his day; he was asked by King George's trainer to ride in the Gold Cup. I couldn't believe my ears when he told us. We had to explain it to Berty – I don't think he understood what the Gold Cup was but Kev waffled about it for so long I think Berty felt he had run it himself by the time the conversation had ended!"

Murtyl yawned again, her eyes getting heavier. "Just a little while longer then I am going to have to get some beauty sleep!"

Nick folded his arms up and rested his head

on them, gazing into her eyes and watching her rosy lips move – he felt like he was with her in these adventures, the way she described them to him. "You are an amazing lady Murtyl, you're truly inspiring! I don't know how you do it."

Murtyl looked over at him and winked. "Not all me, I couldn't have done most of the things I have done without Berty! He has been with me through thick and thin, that man. My life would be nothing without him in it!"

Nick at this point wondered if Berty was still alive, but then thought, well he couldn't be alive otherwise he would be in the house and he would have met him already. He didn't interrupt Murtyl with his thought and let her continue.

"Anyway, when Kevin told me about how he got into the horse riding career and working alongside King George the Fifth with his horses, under the royal trainer Mr. Fulke Walwyn, he gave Berty and me a right old earful about the Gold Cup! It must have been a jolly good experience for him;

sure sounded like it, the way he was talking. I got Kevin to talk me through the race just a few years ago and recorded it on to a Dictaphone. You want to listen to it then? It goes on for a few minutes if you're interested."

"Of course Murtyl; I'd love to!" Nick eyes lit up once again and his ears pricked up ready for it to start.

Murtyl pressed the buttons on the Dictaphone and Kevin Mooney's voice started to come out of the speaker. Kevin's voice came through clearly and precisely with its Lambourn roll and went like this:

I was approached to ride in the spring to ride one of King George Fifth's horses in the Whitbread Gold Cup at Sandown. My horse was Special Cargo, who was trained by the royal trainer, Mr Fulke Walwyn.

I was very excited about the chance to ride the horse for King George the Fifth as it was at one of his favourite courses and Special Cargo had won there four times before, so he knew his way around. His good, quick jumping suited the track as well as the fences that came together very quickly down the back straight. However, there would be another obstacle to contend with: the favourite in the race, Diamond Edge, was from the same stable - a horse that had won the Whitbread Gold Cup twice before - and so was going for his third. Both horses, especially Diamond Edge, suffered badly with leg injuries; this had kept them off the track for the last two seasons. They were trained to the minute in the weeks leading up to the race. The ground had been drying out, which was a problem for Special Cargo with his fragile legs, as he preferred soft ground. However Diamond Edge loved good, fast ground. There was a chance that Special Cargo might not run if no rain came. As it was, it did not! As the race got closer King George the Fifth and Mr. Walwyn decided that Special Cargo should take his chance.

On the day of the race, I rode out first lot at Mr Walwyn's just to calm my nerves; this was the biggest chance of my riding career. After riding out, I cycled home. On the short journey I kept riding the race in my head over and over again, hoping that the horse would handle the fast ground - he might not like it, but at least it would be on the track he loved.

Soon it was time to set off to Sandown Park. Travelling with me in the motor car provided was my wife, Sharon, and my father. They tried to fill me with confidence.

We arrived at Sandown about an hour before the first race. It was a very hot day and the crowd was massive. In the weighing room there was a real buzz; my nerves were getting to me! The valet who looked after the jockeys had all our tack and silks hanging ready. Mine were the famous blue and buff colours with black cap with gold tassels.

It was time to get ready. Just to put the royal colours on was a real privilege and an honour for a local lad born and bred in Lambourn. With the royal colours on it was time to weigh out and get some advice from Mr. Fulke Walwyn. In the weighing room there was excitement, nerves and talk about how the race might be run, between the other jockeys. The bell then rang and it was time to go out to the paddock and meet the royal party with Special Cargo.

On arriving in the paddock, King George the Fifth and Mr. Walwyn put me at ease straightaway by saying, "Just enjoy the occasion. Have a safe ride, but if Special Cargo is not enjoying the fast ground, just look after him."

Both horses looked magnificent in the sun-split sky and the huge crowd really got behind King George the FIfth and wanted him to do well. Nerves were taking over when the bell rang for jockeys to mount; once on his back all was calm. In the parade before the race, Special Cargo was bouncing and felt really well under me.

Soon we were at the start. Three miles and five furlongs, two and a half circuits of Sandown and twenty six fences to jump on fast ground. We were called to make a line and soon we were racing to the first. My plan was to be handy; up in the first three or four all the way. Equally, Diamond Edge was up there as well.

The first circuit went to plan. However, on passing the stands for the final circuit the pace began to quicken and Special Cargo was beginning to lose his place on the fast ground. But still his jumping was quick, so I felt if we could keep in touch, we still had a chance of running well, if not winning. Halfway down the back, Diamond Edge had taken up the running and was jumping well on the hard ground. Turning out of the back straight Special Cargo was only seventh but was slowly getting back to the leaders. Jumping the pond fence (the third last) we saved ground by keeping to the rail; coming off the turn we were in fifth place and starting to close. If we could jump the second to last well, we would be close enough to get placed. We got too close, but we managed not to lose the vital momentum you need for the uphill finish.

At the last there were three in a line, with Diamond Edge in the middle. We were back in fourth - but with a good jump at the last, and quickly into his stride, we would be right there with a chance of winning! With all four horses and jockeys riding for the line, it went to a three-way photograph. The excitement from the crowd was overwhelming - they had just witnessed probably one of the best finishes of the Whitbread Gold Cup ever!

On the long way back to the paddock there had been no announcement of the result. When we had nearly reached the unsaddling enclosure it came. The winner's name boomed out of the loud speakers - it was Special Cargo who had won by a short head in front of Diamond Edge. Unsaddling Special Cargo and waiting for King George the Fifth to arrive, tears of joy were welling in my eyes; the horse with the delicate legs had overcome the fast ground and had carried himself faster than the other eleven horses.

When King George the Fifth arrived in the winning enclosure with Mr. Walwyn, the excitement was overwhelming for everyone. After weighing in, Sharon, my father and I were invited to the royal box to talk through the race with King George the Fifth at length.

Three weeks after the race the yard was still buzzing with excitement when we received a 'phone call from Windsor Castle: King George the Fifth was to have a private dinner party in London, at the home of Colonel Whitbread and his wife, for ten people. In the first conversation it was for myself, my wife, Bill Smith (Diamond Edge's jockey) and his wife to attend, but unfortunately one week before the dinner party was to take place the 'phone rang again, asking if our wives could drop out as the King wanted to invite his children.

The Whitbread was the last ride for Bill Smith as he retired on that day and I then became the number one jockey for Mr. Fulke Walwyn and King

George the Fifth, on the strength of the Special Cargo ride.

"What did you think to that then?" Murtyl waited for Nick's response.

"Brilliant, just brilliant! By golly it must have been a real honour to ride one of the King's horses and win the Gold Cup! Bet he had a whale of a time that day, one he will never forget I'm sure!" Nick exclaimed.

So she continued, "Well, he did teach me a thing or two about how to ride a horse; he also taught me how to catch a wild one and break it in - he made them follow him all over, without any halter on or anything. I used to call him the horse whisperer - it was a running joke we had. It was magical. Still to this day I don't know how he did it. He was very fair but firm with them and they seemed to have a mutual agreement with him - they treated him as if he was at the top of their pecking order."

'Before we knew it Berty was called to Elvington in York on a mission…" Murtyl paused and took a deep breath.

Nick didn't know what to expect next. "Was it bad news Murtyl? The mission - did he succeed?"

Murtyl had a tear in her eye at this point but she managed to swallow the lump in her throat and carried on telling Nick what happened - after all he needed to know so he could write about it all when she had gone.

"Well, he went over to the German and French borders; he was attacking there and was shot down. The lads thought they spotted parachutes come from his Halifax but no one could verify if he was alive, a prisoner of war or if he was on the run. Berty had no family left, just me! His mother and father were imprisoned by the French police under the Vichy government, who were instructed by the Gestapo, and later murdered by them – he was devastated when he got the news. I think a part of him wanted revenge. I don't know how he managed to stay calm - I think that is why we both worked well together. I was a bit of a hothead in my time and he seemed to be the only one who could hold it all together for me. There will never be another like him, one in a million. When I got word that he was missing, I needed a way to get to France, to try and find him. We seemed to feel each other's pain, fear and trouble so I knew in my heart, Berty was in trouble but I knew he couldn't be dead!" Murtyl looked up at him; she had a tear in her eye.

"You don't have to tell me today, you know, Murtyl - if you don't feel like speaking about it anymore, shall we talk about something else?"

Murtyl piped up, "It was a sad time lad. I still had contacts through my father, from Jack Butler and from some of the earlier interviews. So I spoke to them and ended up joining. Because I could speak a few languages, I was offered a desk job at Bletchley Park. I refused the job then and told a few people of my intentions; would they know of any active service that could use me? You see, I was willing to train to whatever level, at whatever capacity, to get to Berty. I never told them the full story of course – I just told them what they needed to know! I kept the real reasons to myself; I didn't want them to decline my offer. Anyway I eventually got to the Special Operations Executive people and was offered the opportunity to train. Once trained, I would be re-assessed and then maybe I would become operational."

Murtyl continued, "I had to undergo tests and training programmes which were difficult for some of their highly trained officers – even they failed some of them – but I passed them all with flying colours. They put me through hell and back." Murtyl started to smile, thinking of the things she had to go through. "It was a crazy time - I would have done anything to find Berty and that was only the start; the worse was yet to come. We were trained in camouflage, detection, evasion and hand-to-hand combat - in which I had an advantage! We also did safe-cracking and breaking; burglary, how to survive in different terrains, how to blend in and go unnoticed in almost any situation. We were given exercises at training camps - we could be dropped somewhere in the country with no money and told to get back in the shortest possible time!"

Murtyl gulped a few sips of tea down. "The trouble was you had no ID papers, money or food rations. I was only beaten once by a guy who I later found out had been dropped in an area he knew really well. He had stayed with an old university mate, had some really good food then the cheating bugger was given a lift back to the training camp gates. Murtyl yawned. "I'm sorry, I'm going have to go to bed now, up early for tomorrow!"

Nick looked over at her, wiping his eyes. "Okay Murtyl! Don't let me keep you; I have some errands to run tomorrow so I'll have to be off at five thirty in the morning. I hope this is not a problem."

As Murtyl stood up to go to upstairs to bed, she smiled at Nick and replied, “No problem at all - go as you please. Hope you get some sleep. Sweet dreams!”

They both headed for their beds. Nick’s head was racing with all the information that had been crammed into his brain that evening – he was so happy that Murtyl trusted him enough to open up to him and was looking forward to hearing some more.

Four thirty the next morning soon arrived. Nick’s alarm woke him up; he had slept well! Rubbing his eyes and stretching he sprang out of bed and made his way to the bathroom to wash his face and brush his teeth. Walking back to his bedroom, he noticed that Murtyl’s bedroom door was open and the bed was made. He smiled to himself at how organised she was and went to get dressed ready to face the day. It was a cold morning so he was pleased he had packed his fleece and extra vests to layer up.

He looked through the window as he passed it to walk down the stairs and noticed that there was a robin on the tree outside the house – he knew winter was on its way and knew he wouldn't see Murtyl as much once the bad weather started, as it was too dangerous to travel on the bike. He rushed downstairs to see what she was up to but she wasn't there.

There was a note on the table. Nick picked this up and it read, "Sorry to abandon you - I had a few jobs to do. I will be back this afternoon if you are about! Drive safe - PS: hope you're layered up, it is cold out!"

He started his bike up at five twenty am, the engine growling more than usual with the dip in temperatures. He let her engine warm up before setting off to run his errands. He felt the cold hit his knees as he took the corners with speed on his bike, and he felt the temperatures through his gloves, making his hands go numb.

When Nick got home he returned to his

normal routines and back to work, tinkering with his race bike but always having Murtyl's life in the back of his mind. He kept asking himself questions like, what the hell had she been into and really done in her life? She was full of common sense, could poach, build, rebuild, shoot, drive and ride with the best of them - she was like some sort of machine. What the blinking heck was she? Questions were running through his head: who really knew her, or more precisely, why did nobody really know or visit her? The Hardys, Webby and all the people he knew through racing, he could not talk to! There was no way to research anything either; Nick had already spent time in the libraries looking at newspapers to see if there were any references to any of the stories Murtyl had told him about – not because he thought she was lying, but because he wanted to go into more depth and see what she was really up to. He soon realised he was not going to find anything and the whole thing was pointless. But he knew he had met the most direct, knowledgeable, bright, intelligent pretty woman in his whole life. He just hoped that in the future he would meet a girl that had half of Murtyl's poise and attributes and if he did he knew he would be a lucky man!

Nick carried on learning more from Murtyl when they had their ride-outs, drive-outs or were doing maintenance. He even spoke to her over coffee, dinner or when out shooting and poaching. Nick knew he had to get as much information from Murtyl as possible whenever she was talking and while she was about. He learnt so much about how to handle himself and about life as well as his own unexplored abilities, but rarely any more stories about Murtyl's life. It was becoming a really big problem with Nick's boss and to be honest it meant there would be no job soon. This was a real worry for Nick; he could not approach Murtyl with his problem - it would not be the honourable thing to do. All he wanted to know was how and when would she trust him enough to at least give him something more to go on.

Nick had a heavy night out with his mates and although he had suggested to Murtyl he would visit on the Saturday he just was not in the mood. Neither of them had a telephone so he just left it, and thought he would ride across to Hutton Rudby on the Sunday. Feeling a little guilty he slept badly on the Saturday night.

Up and off in the morning, he arrived in an hour. Nick quickly parked up and knocked on her front door. To his surprise there was no answer.

After a short while he went round the back, asking Steve, the chef of the Wheatsheaf, if he had seen Murtyl about. He said he hadn't. Once round the back, he saw the garage was locked up as well as the back door. Nick was bothered by this; he knocked loud enough to wake her. She must be up! Hell, it was after nine in the morning!

After no joy at the house, Nick walked up to the shop and looked around but she wasn't there either. Coming back down the village over the green he noticed the lounge curtains were closed. He froze for a moment, concerned there was something wrong. He ran back towards the house, noticing that the bedroom curtains were open, but not the lounge. This might have been something and nothing for some people but not Murtyl - it was tardy and not like her at all. Nick's concern increased but he didn't really know what to do. He knocked again but to no avail. He spied down the edge of the curtains and could just make out there was a light on. This really started the alarm bells ringing in his head, but he still didn't know what to do.

Instinct took over. His stomach churned and he knew there was no time to waste. He went through the front door, literally! He hit it hard with his shoulder a few times with no result, but he knew he had to get in so bugger it; he rode his Kawasaki straight through her front door. He wasn't worried about the bike at this point; it could be fixed later! He dragged his bike back out, kicked the rest of the door in and rushed into the house.

Nick called her name but there was no reply, nothing at all. He knew she could sometimes be in her own little world singing to herself as she pottered about the house, but he still felt that something was very wrong. He turned right into the lounge and clocked the settee; he dropped to his knees and started to cry. Murtyl was peacefully laid on the red settee in her best blouse and skirt, reading glasses on with a letter over her chest.

Once he had gathered his composure Nick went over, knowing she had left some time yesterday, as she was cold. He gently took the letter and read it through his watering eyes. It was from a monastery in western France. It read:

Dear M,

It is with great regret that I have to inform you your great friend Albert Noir has passed away. He left peacefully in his sleep.

Please accept our deepest sympathy and

understand that if there is anything you would like from his belongings or records it is yours. We understand he has no living relatives or associations with anybody except yourself. All details and diaries will be forwarded to you in the next few days.

Albert was a great asset to all who dwell here, and we do understand the two of you worked extremely well together.

Please send no more financial assistance; Albert has only ever been an asset to us as you have been. If you could visit once more we will all choose to see you.

Thank you and bless you,

Charles Andrew Stuart Hobson.

As ever CASH to you.

P.S. I found this note from Berty.

Murtyl, My dear sweetheart,

I have just recovered from a stroke and lost the use of my left arm. I can never apologise enough for what I have put you through, now I have regained my feelings. The blockage of blood flow to parts of my brain must have caused an increase in pressure elsewhere within the cortex. The result is, I now remember!

I have failed you in the most important area of life. I know you loved me, but I was unable to feel or to know what love is. I have no excuse. I know you and Charles did everything you could to help me - except bang me on the bloody head!

All my emotional faculties have been reborn.

My dear, I love you with all my heart. Please accept my deepest apologies, and know, as I leave shortly, that I will be with you forever to support and protect you in every way, everyday.

All my Love,

Berty X

Nick read through the letters again and began to understand some of what must have taken place. He surmised she must have received the letter late yesterday morning and sat down to read it in the evening. Once comprehending the contents, grief and sadness must have taken over as she lay there and she must have left as her will to live subsided. The medical definition would be for a Coroner; at the moment he just needed to call the authorities.

Nick went upstairs and acquired a blanket, came back down and gently placed it over this wonderful lady. Leaving the house he secured the front door in the best way he could and went to see Jo. He used the telephone and called the police.

When this was done, Nick sat outside Murtyl's front door with his head in his hands for a few moments, then pulled himself together and waited for the police to take over, to do whatever they had to do. Nick had replaced the letter on her chest, then run over and over it in his mind wondering how she must have felt, all the time regretting the fact he had not bothered to visit her yesterday. Nick cried once more and felt guilty!

Once the Police arrived Nick gave a statement then was asked to leave; there was nothing he could do. They would arrange for the property to be secured and all the services to be cut off. The rest would be up to the Coroner. If they wanted to talk to Nick they had his address. He went home pretty damn well unhappy with himself, the situation and his guilt. His mind was filtering through every word in the letters; he was going over and over it in his head. Nick knew he had to get home as soon as possible because he was in no fit state to be on the road; his dearest friend and mentor had passed away. He felt a void! Nick knew he would miss Murtyl's presence in his life dearly.

Chapter 7: Descent and Rescue

The weekend dragged; it felt like time was standing still. He was in a nightmare where every minute felt like hours and Nick's head felt as if it would explode at any point.

Monday back into the office and the first thing Nick felt he had to do was tell his boss. This was done and he was told to take a few days off and dig into everything, as there was a story there and he didn't seem to have it. Nick did as he was told and went home. Looking through his notes there was nothing he could go on, no facts that were provable, just her word which he totally believed in. Nick, however, had no proof of the life she may have led; he was in a situation now, as he didn't know what the hell he was to do.

After a few days he went back and fronted up; he spoke the truth to his boss, Bill. "I have nothing sir! I know what she did tell me, I know what she showed me and what she could do, but I have no way of putting all these things into context with her life. I know about Mr. Noir in France but he has passed away too”.

The answer Nick got in return did not surprise him in the least; his boss was not very sympathetic and said, “You know where the door is, and you must have some leads to chase up. You either have something or you don’t. Your P45 will be here to pick up in fourteen days. I’ve had enough of the long leash I gave you!”

Nick sighed. He had had enough of all the aggravation he was getting, and decided he wasn’t bothered anymore. He walked out of the door and closed it behind him - he didn’t feel like arguing at the moment and he certainly wasn’t in the mood to be getting locked up for damaging property. So he left in silence, without a fuss, like he had never been there.

Nick left the office and couldn’t be bothered to empty the few things out of his desk drawers. He shrugged his shoulders and forgot about it; to him at the moment life might as well be over. He kept his word to Murtyl and never said a thing to anyone about anything she told him. Bugger he was in a hole! Nick knew it wouldn't take three weeks before he'd have to go back to his parents with his tail between his legs – he knew this whole thing was just impossible. He started suffering from depression - he stayed in his flat for a few days; he didn't get dressed, shaved or washed and tried to think of a way to move forward with it all. He decided he would call the police in an effort to at least do something.

The sergeant answered the phone and said to Nick, "I'm sorry son; there is nothing you can do at the moment. You are just going to have to leave it with us." The police wanted another statement and then Murtyl's solicitor would arrange the house clearance once the Coroner was satisfied – until then, unless he was needed sooner, Nick had to just sit there and twiddle his thumbs. They never called.

Nick seemed to lose track of time. He suddenly realised that he was doing something Murtyl had never done - he was letting his life waste away as he moped about something he couldn't change. He had a long shower, had a nice clean shave and made himself look presentable. Running over to the calendar Nick saw he had missed the Coroner's hearing and the next thing was the funeral. He was very nervous and sad at the same time.

The 20th January arrived and sure enough, out of respect and love, Nick got to the service. He thought only he and one or two others would be there. Jobless and not too enthusiastic about life he sat there in silence, his thoughts and feelings all over the place. He started watching mysterious people arriving in limousines and entering the church where Murtyl lay. They were all in suits - very flashy suits at that, and they seemed to come in pairs. There was no pattern to the pairs; some males, some male and female and some just females. Nick now had more questions running through his head: who the hell were these people? Why were they at his dearest friend's funeral? Why did he not know of them and why did Murtyl never speak of them? What did they want?

After frowning for a few moments and getting angry at the thought of someone taking all Murtyl's assets from her, he realised that these people were from governments - diplomat types. He knew they wore 'that kind of cut' suits and clothing. Nick then noticed they were of different nationalities; he could tell as each pair talked to each other and acknowledged other pairs. This was really odd, so much so that he watched and listened.

The service was short; it seemed to be over before it started really and then the body was taken to the crematorium but nobody was supposed to go. Murtyl's ashes would be with her true love, but the whereabouts of that was not to be told! Nick really was getting his head into a spin at this; surely there was no issue in knowing where her ashes were to lie - why couldn't he go and see them together - just once - to say his final goodbyes to his friend? Nick remembered Murtyl telling him about where Albert was and the name of the Monastery.

As the procession of people left after paying their respects, most of them laid wreaths by the door. They were all beautiful; most were small, but the cards nearly all read the same way. There was a national flag, a year or two years named and a very simple message in their own language. Nick made a note of what was on the cards to translate them. They read:

The freedom and stability of our nation can partly and directly be attributed to the action you took on our behalf. We will, as people, forever be in your debt. Thank you.

Nick's mind was just in a blur. He tried to talk to

some of the mysterious pairs about the cards, but he was just ignored. He saw his boss, who just shrugged his shoulders as if to say, now you can see what you could have uncovered, yet you failed. Nick didn't know whether to be angry or whether to cry at this point. He was in such a state - his motivation was non-existent and Murtyl wasn't there to help him through the rough times ahead!

Nick left the service more confused than ever and the depression just kept getting worse. No job meant the bikes had to be sold; the flat had gone and this meant he had no bed of his own. All that there was for him to do, was to sign on, then to start looking for jobs – fast.

Nick went for interviews. He knocked on doors; offered to work for nothing for a month to prove he was good enough. The answers were all the same: we can't insure you to do that, you have no experience. The list went on; it was all a big nightmare. To top it all off, the girlfriend he thought he had, decided to leave too. Was life worth bothering with? Life just kept spiralling in on itself. People he had known for years, even from school, looked at him as if he was a stranger. He had lost weight, aged and his skin had a grey pallor to it. He really was in a state! Nick's family didn't really bother with him; they got on with their lives and just ignored his health and wellbeing - not even offering to help or listen. He started to clean windows and cut grass for people in the neighbourhood, not taking payment even when they offered. He did it just to stay sane.

After around four months a letter arrived through the letterbox. It had bounced round a few addresses, including his ex-employers, and eventually arrived at his mother's home. Nick opened it - after all it was addressed to him. It seemed to be from a solicitor in Yarm. Yarm was a market town near to Hutton Rudby. Nick unfolded the letter and started to scan through it. What on earth had he got wrong now, he wondered! It read:

Dear Mr. Nick,

Would you please make contact with us, and make an appointment with Mr. Ron Kirk as soon as possible.

Nick found the contact number at the bottom of the letter and gave him a call straight away. The following week was the earliest Mr. Kirk was going to be available. Mr. Kirk would not disclose any information to Nick over the 'phone, and said he would only release information in person. If Nick wanted to know what the solicitor had contacted him for, he would have to make an appointment and visit. He did so!

Wearing the best suit he had and borrowing his mother's car, Nick travelled to Yarm looking for the solicitor's offices. It didn't take him long; he soon found them, close to the market centre. He entered the gleaming white building and walked over some really thick carpet, seeing eyes peering at him. He asked for Mr. Kirk at the reception desk, and was directed to a chair. He sat down, waiting and wondering what this was all about.

Once Mr. Kirk had finished speaking to his last client, Nick was asked to enter his office. The office was plush, with an old fashioned green light on a large, dark oak desk with green leather inlay. The carpet was deep and in Nick's opinion was far too good for an office – his mother didn't even have this sort of quality carpet at home, never mind in an office. The walls were hidden with deep, dark bookcases full of legal books and there were a few files on the floor. Nick shook Mr. Kirk's hand and saw that he was a pleasant, smiling, happy sort of chap. Mr. Kirk was slight of build, with grey hair and side parting and gold rimmed glasses. The most interesting thing was that he seemed to be happy, always smiling - Nick just was not quite sure how to take this. The whole unemployment, no future, down and out things were really taking their toll and what the hell had he done wrong now? Nick was offered coffee and asked several questions about himself: his date of birth, where he used to live and what the registration was of the GPZ 550 that he had sold. He proffered this information, then he was told that this was to do with a promise he had made.

Nick at this point raised his voice slightly. “I never go back on my word and if I owe someone some money, it will be paid back as soon as I can find work Mr. Kirk!” Nick started to get worried; whom did he owe money to? He couldn’t put a name to any person - he thought he was debt free.

Mr. Kirk piped up, “Settle and relax. This is nothing to do with you owing money; I have been asked to do this on behalf of a client as their last wish and I just had to be sure I was talking to the correct person. I am now satisfied and will get on with business!” Nick was confused and then looked over in the direction Mr. Kirk was heading. What the hell was he up to?

Mr. Kirk then pulled some papers from the

safe hidden behind him and gently placed them on his desk. He spoke in a soft tone but a serious one. "This, young man is a contract between the deceased and you. The firm I represent is working on behalf of the deceased, and will oversee this contract to its fruition. This may be after I pass away but the responsibility will be handed on to another partner within the firm until it is fulfilled. Would you sign here please? My secretary will witness it."

Nick was about to respond when Mr. Kirk went back to his safe and pulled out a pile of diaries. Nick was then mesmerised and stuttered, "T-they aren't M-Murtyl's diaries, are they?"

Mr. Kirk smiled. "You get this one to look at for three minutes; it is dated June 1944 to October 1945. It should, if you're as bright as I am told you are, give you a chance to read quite a lot of this."

Nick took the diary with both hands and glanced at the first ten pages then burst into tears, handing the diary back to Mr. Kirk. He handed Nick a tissue and then said, “My name is Ron and I’m here to help you with this, but you have to make the decision regarding your word to this lady.”

Nick replied straight away without thinking. “Of course I want to write up that wonderful lady’s life; she told me so much and yet at the same time it all seemed to be a fantasy. The only things that were concrete were the skills she displayed, the pictures on the walls and her car and bike, but the things she told me were just hinting at something I know nothing of.”

Ron replied, “Yes Nick but it is all in her diaries! I can help you do the research you will need - as time passes more information will become common knowledge and it will get easier. The bones are in the diaries but you can’t have them without the contract being signed. Even then you will only get one at a time, as they must be followed progressively, and by her instruction. My instructions are to keep this informal and to be by your side as and when required; help you with any legal issues and give you clear advice regarding time issues where the Official Secrets Act is concerned."

Well that was Nick hooked. "If you are able, and have been instructed, then I have to do it, for Murtyl!"

Ron smiled and while handing the ink pen over to Nick said, "Just sign here." Nick took the pen carefully; it felt like a light had come on in the very dark life he was currently in.

He signed on the dotted line very neatly considering his hand was shaking and asked Ron another question. "What happens next sir? Do I get to take the first one home with me?"

"No Nick you do not; there are other things to deal with first," Ron replied, answering his question clearly.

Ron's secretary witnessed the signature and left the room quickly before anything was mentioned in the room.

Ron was the first to speak. "Right Nick, your

living situation is not really satisfactory at present and I need to know where you are and what you're doing, so you will be needing these." As Ron bent down towards a drawer he was opening, he held up some keys and handed them to Nick.

"What are these for?" Nick asked.

Ron told him, "They are for our friend Murtyl's home; you are to use the house until you no longer need to. You cannot sell any of the contents but you may replace and refurbish as required. I know your present financial position and to help you cope there is enough provision to cover the rates, poll tax and all utilities for eighteen months. Again I repeat: you may never borrow against the property and upon your death it goes back into her estate. Murtyl believed this would be enough for you to have a chance in life. She was concerned she had taken this away, while assessing your trustworthiness and abilities to do as she has asked."

Nick by this time was too dumbstruck to

speak or move. After a few minutes he pulled himself together and although still shaking, leant forward and dived for the waste paper basket. He wretched and threw up!

Ron then ushered him out, assisted Nick to his mother's car and said, "Relax Nick, I expect you to be in your new home within a week and I want to see you here in two weeks' time at the same time. I know there are some time issues with some of this stuff, so we need to be careful about how quickly or slowly each of the diaries may be worked on. Most importantly we need to find you secure work as your confidence has taken a battering."

Nick moved into Murtyl's home and settled in very quickly. All the people in the village he had met through Murtyl were extremely happy to have him there.

He settled in and kept looking for work. He visited Mr. Kirk as per the agreement, and Ron started to help him with some delivery and filing work. This helped Nick and he carried on applying for work all over.

To ease some of the strain, Ron threw Nick another set of keys one spring afternoon. He said, "I can now see why Murtyl trusted you. Here are a set of keys for her garage and her bike. I have made sure you are insured for it. At least this way you have some transport. Look after it for her, won't you?" Nick was gobsmacked again and so grateful. Ron then carried on. "Another thing son – you'd better have the keys for the Healey; she needs to be turned over once in a while, and it would break Murtyl's heart to think she was not being looked after. Mind you are not insured for her, so you cannot take her out on the road. That will come in a few years. You OK with that?" Nick as ever was humbled and emotional about the help he continued to receive from Murtyl.

Over the next few years he found solid work and settled down with a local girl. He stayed in touch with Ron and they became friends, meeting out of office hours for a chat and coffee every three or four months. This kept Ron abreast of Nick's status and how life was progressing. They talked of Murtyl often but never mentioned the diaries and Nick's promise. It was just agreed that when the time came, Nick would receive the first one.

Chapter 8: The First Diary

A package arrived in the post nine years after Murtyl's demise almost to the day. Addressed to Nick from Ron Kirk, a brief note was attached which read:

Dear Nick,

Not seen you for a short while. I trust all is well. It is time for you to deliver on your promise! Please research Diary One and come to me with your results. I will help with publishing once I have been through all with you.

Best Regards,

Ron.

NB Diary written post WW2.

Nick went up to his office and started to read. He read it through and chuckled to himself. "No bloody wonder you couldn't talk to me. If I can verify any of this through the Internet, then the world has a right to know who you bloody well were."

A letter was tucked into the back of the diary addressed to Nick. He opened it and saw from the handwriting it was from Murtyl. It read as follows:

Dear Nick,

If you have this letter then I have already had to leave one way or another. Ron Kirk will guide you through some things to keep you on the correct side of certain authorities. The diaries are written post-action, as it could not be done during an operation. They are an outline, and you will, through research, have to verify a number of things.

However I would like to explain why I have chosen you to take this task on.

I first met you in June, 1967. I was the lady who arrived one night - you woke up in your cabin on the super tanker 'Arabiya' with me in your bunk. You were only four. We got on really well, and we tended to leave your older brother and sister to it. In the few days I was on board we struck up a friendship. Your father, Captain Nigel Pearson, accepted me on board as an escape route from the work I had been doing prior to the Suez Crisis. I am sure you remember a little!

My exit route had been compromised. I was able to get to the Arabiya as she was only one hundred nautical miles away from the Suez entrance in the Mediterranean, half a day's steaming behind her sister ship. She was caught up in the crisis. You may recall our daily lifeboat drills and me pointing out to you various military things such as submarine periscopes, jets and helicopters all around us. After steaming up and down the Med., we were discharged in Sicily with your mother, brother and sister to fly to Rome and on to the UK. Do you remember your brother being in trouble for dawdling and having chewing gum sticking his short pants together? Well I put it there to keep people's attention on him and away from me. You, bless you, took on the role of being my charge and we flew through all customs and immigration. Even at the tender age of four I became indebted to you.

I have watched you from a distance over the years and looked upon you as the child I never had. I have seen you racing in the Shell Oils Championships with Geoff Towers, Alan Stewart, Dave Woolams and the rest. I have listened to their views on you and am proud to know of their respect for you.

This is why I have chosen you to do this for me; I know you will not let me down.

Be strong and be the best of the best. I will always be with you.

Love,

Murtyl.

Diary Entry 1: In with the Baker Street Irregulars

Interviewed by Vera Atkins for F section, (French section of the SOE). The flat the interview took take place in was in Orchard Court just off Baker Street in London's West End. All subsequent meetings and briefings were held here. I was never allowed into F section headquarters in Baker Street.

I was greeted by Mr. Park in a dark suit. He never asked names and seemed to know all about me - I assume through MI5 and the mysterious Mr. Potter. I was escorted into the lift through the gilded gates and up to the second floor. He would speak in perfect English or French, whichever I preferred. He ushered me into the flat and straight into the bathroom, which was used as the waiting room as no other space seemed to be available. The first time, waiting in the black and white tiled bathroom, I was a bit nervy. So I sat and relaxed on the edge of the black bath and waited.

Shortly after that Mr. Park took me to meet Mr. Laurence Buckmaster, head of F section. He was slender, tall and athletic with thin, fair hair. He was relaxed and introduced himself with a firm handshake. His only comment was, "We don't ask questions here." With that remark I knew I had a chance.

He then took me off down the corridor and into another room, and introduced me to Miss Atkins. He explained that Miss Atkins would have all, if any dealings with me from now on, and she did. It would seem she had made up her mind regarding my recruitment within a few minutes. We got on really well!
She even saw me personally to my plane for departure to France after training.

I trained at the Thatched Barn under Captain J.Edgar Wills in camouflage, coding and by some bloody magicians to divert the eye while taking the prize. Hand-to-hand combat and assassination training was at Arisag in Scotland. Un-armed combat training was with Willie Fairburn and Eric Sykes of the Shanghai Municipal Police; security and tradecraft at Group B School at Beaulieu; demolition techniques and wireless operations at various country houses. Parachute training was with STS 51, at RAF Ringway just outside Manchester.

Entry 2: Delivery of the package

After days of waiting in a safe house just outside London for the weather to clear, the four of us were driven in two separate cars to the classified airfield we were to be dispatched from. We then went through our final checks, just in case we had missed anything: our luggage was meticulously searched, the clothes we wore too, stitch by stitch, pocket by pocket. Anything, absolutely anything that could link you to the allies or Britain had to go. If part of a cinema ticket was in a pocket, it could result in torture, and a quick execution. One of the others, it would seem, had not been supplied with French footwear. Even though the footwear was well used, they ripped out the inner soles and sanded the leather between the heel and the ball of the foot to remove any maker's imprint. The enemy knew the difference in the construction of a shoe made in Britain and France! Even the polish on our shoes had to be right - French waxes were different enough to have you caught. The others were going to another cell; they would be working loosely together, in different jobs for the same network. They could acknowledge each other and progress their cover stories. I was going in alone, with my own cover story to remember.

Vera Atkins, second in command for the SOE (F section), handed each of us a cyanide capsule, with a very solumn face. We all thanked her. Vera then advised us she would see all our signals and work. She looked forward to our return and debriefing us. She was always positive.

We boarded the four-engined bomber, a Stirling designed in America. It was 0125hrs. Dark, with a moon that was no more than a quarter full.

161 Squadron flew Stirlings; they specialised in this sort of operation, dropping persons of counterintelligence and some propaganda leaflets behind enemy lines. On this occasion they had to drop leaflets and three personnel somewhere in the Normandy and Brittany regions, then head northwest to drop me. This leg of the journey would take an hour and a half.

Roughly twenty five minutes to go, we were attacked. I'm not sure what kind of aeroplane it was - probably an ME 110 night fighter that fell lucky on a lone allied aeroplane. Stirlings were quick when on full throttle and could outrun most German aircraft, but being caught at a cruise speed of just under two hundred knots we were sitting ducks. The cover of darkness had not worked out for us and we were strafed right along the fuselage. The pilot threw her all over, climbing, diving, rolling in a bid to evade our attacker. The airframe made stress tearing and cracking sounds above the engines and wind noise. The pilot could not compete in this crate with a fighter, but he tried, and bloody hard. The navigator was strapped in; my handler -- a sergeant - and I just had to brace ourselves where we could. My parachute harness was unbearably tight and with the parachute behind me on its tethers as I had been using it to sit on, I couldn't get my backside on to anything. I ended up lying on the floor with my arms and legs spread out under the benches, wedged into the sharp spars of the fuselage. The strapping around my lower limbs (to protect my ankles as I was jumping in shoes suitable for Paris life) was tight, making my legs and feet feel numb, like blocks of wood, which made it even harder to get that vital purchase on the surfaces inside the violently moving aircraft. The smell of fuel became quite overpowering inside the fuselage; at least one fuel line or tank was punctured. It took all my strength not to become a loose object clattering around the fuselage like a rag doll.

The dark had to be on our side - the pilot just needed to find cloud cover, if only for just a few minutes. We had to be somewhere north of the Central Massive, and there weren't too many fighter aircraft bases in that area. The Jerry couldn't have that much fuel; he would have to disengage at some point. We raced for cloud. The fighter had one last burst, ripping through the fuselage. His spent ammunition also went up through our cockpit.

We started to climb hard. Our angle of attack was too great - the engines started to lose their purchase on the air and we decelerated. The fighter pilot must have seen this and left the action, presumably to go and register his kill. The Stirling stalled, heeled slightly to starboard then started to dive. The engines began to scream as they were unable to keep up with the speed we were now gaining in the dive. I fell forward and took a few nasty knocks here and there, on the way toward the cockpit. Several screens were blown out and the cockpit was a bloody mess!

The pilot and co-pilot had been slaughtered. The navigator and I were left. I still don't even know if we had a rear gunner, never mind if the poor bugger had survived or not. We hauled what was left of the bodies out of their seats, then I took control. We were not in a spin, but we were rolling which made orientation relatively difficult. The altimeter was reading just over five thousand feet. I throttled back while feathering the props as she buffeted. Numb feet on the rudder pedals, I started to try and pull her out of the dive, while rolling the yoke in the opposite direction to the roll with a little left rudder. I was screaming at the navigator to give me a hand on the other yoke. He may have only delayed for a few seconds prior to doing as instructed, but it seemed like an age as I fought and strained. Eventually she responded and started to bring her nose up.

Once we started to gain height and we were out of the roll, the engines settled, propellers pitched correctly, we started to climb steadily. We had been as low as twelve or thirteen hundred feet - it was pretty touch and go. I could only hope we were still heading in the right direction. The compass seemed to be jammed on a heading; it did not move when I tapped it. Shouting at the navigator I pointed to the zip pocket in my jumpsuit that held my field compass. The instrument panel had taken a few hits. We had no oil pressure readings but the engines were still running - that was positive. We were losing fuel from an outer tank. I made the relevant transfers to the inboard tanks, and locked the cocks off. Wiping blood off the other instruments and controls, I found we had airspeed, false horizon, fuel and the altimeter instrumentation only. I didn't need to check the landing gear as I wouldn't need it. The controls worked well enough - the job was still on!

I instructed the navigator to find a heading for my drop zone, intending to overshoot so that I would be able to turn the Stirling round, setting her on a vector and height that would get her and the navigator back over the UK. His name turned out to be Bill. I could not describe him as it was still dark and we were running on infra-red light. He was covered in blood as I was. I could say he looked terrified. I shouted through the din to look on the bright side; he was alive and going home. He looked at me oddly, then realised he was not going to be allowed to jump with me and protested. I explained gently but firmly that he would jeopardise my mission if he jumped, and I would happily shoot him if he carried on whining. I made a note of his squadron number as well as the name of his home town. I suggested that if he jumped after I had departed, I would hunt his family down and dispatch them on my return to England. I think by that time he was a little punch drunk. Realising I was serious, he then started to pay attention, learning what I had to teach him, to allow him a chance of getting the crate home and survive.

I started to familiarise him with the instruments we had left and the controls. At least as we were up in the air, he didn't have to learn any take off procedures. I only had to go through straight and level, using the bubble as the false horizon as it was dark. He was not as bright as one would have hoped as a student, but maybe he felt under a little pressure, letting his nerves show. A bit slack I thought! I don't know, but once he got the grasp of four throttles and was shown there was enough fuel to get home, he started to sweat a little less. I gave him the yoke to get the hang of it: rotate it clockwise, the aircraft would start to rotate clockwise. This would cause slip and the craft to lose height rapidly, falling to the right. Enter a little left rudder, maintain the height, pull back on the yoke and she would turn to the right. We practised left and right turns several times and his nerves really did start to settle. He started to chat incessantly now - not something I ever appreciate, never mind with that level of noise, while trying to teach the idiot. We then went through throttle back, lose speed and decend, throttle up and gain altitude. The poor bugger was no natural but we got enough done in the half an hour to give him a chance.

I then had to go through engine shut-down procedures and individual fuel cut-off valves above the pilot's seat, just in case he lost an engine or had a fire. If he was attacked I just hoped he would have the guts to go down with her. He would only get one chance at landing, as I had no time to teach or practise go-around procedures. On Stirlings you had to remember that the flaps were operated electrically, but not at the same time as the bomb bay doors which were on the same circuit. I didn't think that was too much of an issue as we were not on a bombing run and carried no explosives that needed to be jettisoned. Then I had to go through descent routines and flaring close to the ground on landing. He would just have to use his own judgment and wing that one. At least he would arrive over the UK as the sun rose; he would be able to see the ground and could use his eyes rather than go in just on instruments. I said tallyho, best of luck, got out of the pilot's seat awkwardly and moved to the rear of the aircraft.

I opened the door after attaching my static line, making sure it was secure, and departed. The tail flew past me as my static line became taut. I was rotating but not rolling as my parachute was deployed. As it opened, my descent was only partially retarded; the canopy had not fully opened. I kicked for all I was worth and eventually, about four hundred feet to go, she fully deployed. I smiled for the first time since leaving England. Covered in blood, soaking with sweat; soon I would be at work. About bloody time too!

My landing in the dark was a tad hard but fine; I rolled sideways as per training and caught a rock with my left shoulder and the ground with my left elbow at the same time. The bump smarted a little as my shoulder dislocated. This was the first time in my life I had received a debilitating injury - never mind being shot at with malice. I thought: so this is what war is all about. OK. Bring it on!

Entry 3: Contact Made

It was not turning out to be one of the best days in my life. I got up and pulled my parachute in as best as I could, knowing I had to move. I was a good way off from my reception party, but there might be a different one waiting for me here after seeing my parachute. Everything collected up, I started to move as briskly as I could with the available moonlight. I needed to find shelter of some sort, a place to check my kit over, send a wireless message confirming I was on French soil and was on the move.

After a mile or two, shelter was found in the form of a wooded area well away from any roads. My compass was in the Stirling on the way to England so map reading was out, even when it was light. Finding a ditch located by a stream, I started to settle. Removing the flight gear and the wrapping from my legs, my body was starting to breathe. Thank the Lord they fed us with steak and eggs prior to departure. If they had not, I would have been in trouble by now. Digging a hole to hide the parachute was too difficult with only one arm, so re-location of the shoulder became the first priority.

The light was coming up as the sun rose. I needed to find a strong branch reaching out from a tree, a little below my shoulder height. It took about ten minutes to find what I was looking for. Rolling up a glove I placed it in my mouth. Lifting my left arm over the branch with my right hand, I allowed the left arm to dangle. I moved my body closer to the branch until my torso was an inch or so away from it. Holding my left arm with my right hand and guiding the ball as close to its socket as possible, I dropped to my knees quickly, using my body weight to create pressure across the branch, acting as a fulcrum and popping the ball back into its socket. My teeth clamped down on the glove, as I writhed on the floor for a few moments. It would be sore, but I was back in action. I waited a few minutes, checking that all the fingers worked correctly on the left arm.There was no great pain. Lucky, lucky, lucky - no trapped nerves!

I washed in the stream, cleansing myself, then rested, hiding until mid-afternoon. It was time to check through my kit, get some bearings and move!

As it happened, when going through my kit, I found my transmitter was trashed, not from the landing but the shells that ripped through it in the aircraft. It was irreparable; the frequency crystals were smashed and there was nothing worth saving - something else that had to be hidden. It meant there would be less to carry and less danger going through checkpoints, which I knew would have to be crossed. My papers were undamaged; I just had to hope they would be valid in the area I had landed. Luck could be on my side yet!

As dusk started to fall I was on the move. I headed in the direction of the setting sun - west, working on the assumption that I had exited the Stirling before we had reached my rendezvous point and headed home. Had Bill made it, or had he chickened out and jumped? He could have been captured and be giving the game away to the enemy right now. Not a happy thought. The Nazis could be homing in on me; I had to move and quickly!

Moving crosscountry, I looked for anything that would give me a clue as to where I was on the map. This part of France was quite flat; just rolling hill after rolling hill. When I came to roads, I followed them to junctions, but just as we had done back home, the direction signs had been taken away. I was going to have to take a risk or two, to get a start. Hearing some approaching engines I took cover. They were twin-cylinder Citroëns running on petrol; they had to be German. Hardly anybody in the country had access to petrol except the Germans. I let them pass and carried on, on foot.

Several more vehicles came by, one or two running on coke gas. They were slow and had to be French. Coke gas would allow an engine to run but it produced little power. If I played my cards right and kept up with this one, it would either take me to a village or at least a farmhouse. It turned out to be a farmhouse.

Observing from a distance from dawn to dusk, I dared not approach until I was sure they had no guests from the military. Keeping an eye on the farm buildings, I made my way to the chicken house and stole a few eggs. Warm from the nest, I tapped them open, one at a time on my teeth and swallowed the contents. I needed the protein; carbs would have to wait for a less dangerous time. Drinking water came from the cattle trough. Then slowly I moved onto the milk parlour roof, where I could get a little sleep and observe my surroundings in the moonlight.

Sure enough the cattle in the fields started to queue at the gates near the dairy parlour at about 0430hrs. The farmer came out and started to perform his milking duties. Once the cows had been milked he cleaned out the byre and went off to tend to his other duties. That milk had to go somewhere. This could be my transport to the nearest village. It was safer to make no contact than to make contact with a German sympathiser.

Around 1100hrs a coke gas fuelled, flatbed truck lumbered its way up to the farm - a rusty old Renault with a little blue paint still hanging on to parts of the cab. The driver got out of the old rust bucket, jumped down onto one leg and limped onto the other. He did not hobble badly and seemed to have a happy air about him. Weathered tan-coloured skin, he wore a washed-out blue shirt with a red neckerchief wrapped around his neck and a British style flat cap. Probably in his forties, he really was so French it was funny.

The driver loaded the dozen or so churns the farmer had left out onto the Renault, as the farmer returned. He was quite chubby, roughly five foot six, his sheep dog clinging to his leg, desperate for its next command. His trousers came up to his chest and were held there with a big-buckled, wide, brown leather belt. He wore wooden-soled shoes and a cream vest. His head was almost bald and he was full of smiles when he saw the Renault driver. They greeted each other and headed to the farmhouse. The farmer's wife came to meet them, a bottle of wine in hand, some cheese and a long loaf of bread she must have baked herself. She was round-faced with red cheeks and grey hair tied up in a bun. A smile as broad as it could be, competed with her backside swaying in a large, tie-dyed green skirt. Her blouse was partially hidden under an old apron covered in flour.

I moved to the blind side of the truck, opening the driver's door as quietly as possible, then started to go through his paper work; his next stop was Rebais. I retired to my hiding place and looked at my silk map; Rebais was about thirty miles northeast of Paris. Bill had not done too bad a job - I was about ten miles away from my original target.

On the back of the Renault, a few wooden boxes were held in place by ropes attached to the cab. I returned to the truck and checked inside them both; one was empty and the other was full of coke to use for fuel. This idea could be stupid and reckless but I needed to find some sort of cover. With what was left of my kit, I climbed into the empty box and waited.

Fifteen minutes later the truck was started and we were on the move. The truck dawdled along at a very sedate pace; I heard the driver shout to a few people as he passed them, telling them he had no time to stop as he had a rendezvous and mustn't be late.

A little later the truck pulled up, the driver got out and opened a gate into a meadow. He drove the truck through the gate and parked up. It sounded then like he had shut the gate behind us. He was leaning against the truck - I heard him fiddle around a little and strike a match and I could smell the smoke from his cigarette as he hummed a tune. I then heard the sound of a bell on a bicycle and a girl shouting the name of Andres, to which he, the driver, answered. They laughed and joked a little, then went a little way into the meadow with a package I assumed must be food. The noises coming from the meadow made me giggle a little; they were having some real fun together - the kind you can only have with your clothes off! I didn't need to see any of it to know he was an experienced man.

When they had finished, they started to eat, talking about the aircraft that had gone over the night before. The Germans tracked the aircraft with radar after it had been attacked. They knew it had been hit, and were trying to work out why it had come over this way, then headed back out. They had not seen me jump from the aircraft. A local farmer had seen something but he would not parley with the Germans. My mind was racing;

could these two be sympathetic to the allies? I listened a while longer. They were exchanging information quietly and it was difficult to hear, but I did hear the phrases fuse wire, and attack! It was time to make a decision: do I reveal myself and ask for help, or do I stay hidden and have no control of what may happen later? Both high risk.

Before I had thought through the dilemma, my body was out of the box and walking toward them. Knife in one hand and pistol in the other, I approached the two, who were making love again. I arrived at the top end so to speak, or at least where the heads were. She was face up, eyes shut, moaning whilst writhing in a rhythm that matched his. Her long, auburn hair was gripped in his fists as he drew her towards him with each energetic thrust of his hips. His breathing getting harder and faster as was hers, I felt I should interrupt before we got to the point of no return!

Tapping her on the shoulder with the knife and cocking the pistol in my right hand inches from his head, I said, “Andres,” firmly. They froze, both looking up at me in terror. They then looked at each other, the sweat beading on their faces. He rolled over so they both lay naked in front of me. I glanced down and said to the girl, “You’re easily pleased I see!” They grabbed some clothes to place in front of themselves. I then asked, “Is there room for another?” That seemed to break the ice nicely and they burst out laughing.

Quickly we got to grips with the fact that they were not in the Resistance but they did do a little courier work. To put me in contact with the Resistance would be difficult and might take a little time. Between them they would hide me - it would mean meeting his wife and possibly her husband. They asked me to be discrete! I suggested we get on and discretion would be my pleasure, then laughed!

I was two days in hiding with the help of Andres and the girl, before I was picked up by two members of the Resistance. There was no need to blindfold me, as I was placed in the boot of their Citroën Traction Avant. This model of car was favoured by the Resistance; it was front-wheel drive, handled very well and was easy to maintain. Access to the boot was from inside the car, which made security for the two men easy, and transporting me not too difficult. They were pretty rough with me, although I did appreciate their dilemma: was I the real deal that should have been with them four or so days ago, or was I a German plant? I had no choice but to trust them, roll up in the boot and enjoy the ride. They had placed some blankets over me and instructed me not to make a sound no matter what. In the end we were never stopped at any checkpoints, which was great - but running through my mind was, how come we had not been stopped?

The car pulled up into a garage that was dark inside. I was asked to get out of the car once it had stopped. As I was exiting the car, my hands were tied behind my back and I was blindfolded. I felt pretty rubbish to be honest; the journey had aggravated my left shoulder and the bruising was really coming out now. I was bundled around a bit then knocked unconscious.

I came round tied to a chair, still blindfolded. It took some time for my mind to clear. I played a little, pretending not to have woken up; I wanted to know what I was in for. Was I with the right people or had I really made a boo-boo?

As it happened I could only hear the French language being spoken. This was a little comforting but I was by no means home and dry yet. The first thing that really hit was the odour of the place; this was no ordinary garage. Yes, there was the smell of leather, oil and the usual petrol smells, but there was something else: the smell was from engines that had been pushed to the limit - that slightly burnt odour so distinctive to racers.Then it dawned on me and I got really quite excited as memories came flooding back. It could not be so, surely! Vera would have told me if the MI5 and 6 had done their job properly. Maybe they had not put two and two together; I don't know. I did know that I needed to hear one or two voices before I let anybody know I was fully awake.

Two more men came in. A hot, bright light shone into my face and the blindfold was ripped off. I blinked, screwing my eyes up. All I could see was the bright light; my interrogators were all standing behind the burning light. One man then came from behind me, placing a pistol barrel to my head and cocking the trigger. They were very serious and wanted to be sure I was authentic, not a German plant. They knocked me about a little and really put some effort into prodding my left shoulder. That did smart; tears were running down my face with the pain. They were going through all my clothes, looking for clues. I only had on my underwear, wondering what they would put me through next.

Then I heard the tone: the commanding,

distinctive voice of the eagle beak- nosed, slicked-back hair World War One fighter ace. My tears became ones of joy and relief as I started to laugh. I shouted to Uncle Robert, "Is Willy here too?" and everything went silent. I then shouted, "You haven't forgotten your favourite niece, have you? The little girl you taught to drive, fly and race? The little girl you bought an Austin Seven for - her first car, Uncle Willy, Uncle Robert - have you?"

Robert replied, "Ma chère, it can't be you! You can't be the precocious little girl we love so much - all grown up, can you?"

"Oh yes, don't you recognise me?"

The silent Willy Grover-Williams then stepped in and freed me. He picked me up and cuddled me. Willy, Robert and I hugged each other and we all leaked a lot from the eyes...

Uncle Willy then looked down at my shoulder and winked. He said, "Ouuuch! Just a moment - Auntie Yvonne makes just the stuff for that!"

He came back a few moments later with a couple of small jars and started to apply the contents of one to my exposed left shoulder. It was sore anyway but with the bashing it had taken from my interrogators it was particularly inflamed and angry.Will then started to speak to me in English in his particularly calming, soothing voice. I felt at home anyway but he revealed to me that his father was the famous horse racing trainer from Berkshire. His mother was French and he had grown up bi-lingual. His style was French - well dressed, in a suit and tie, his hair slicked back, with an oval face with a noble nose. His eyes smiled and and I could see why Auntie Yvonne had fallen for him. His eyes smiled at me full of mischief and he told me a few stories from before the war that I knew nothing of.

He had been quite a tennis player and a lot of the other drivers had no real idea of who he was. He liked it that way! He had started as a chauffeur, attempting to escape from France with a general he was driving for, but failing to get out from Dunkirk. They were trapped and had made their way up to Brittany and escaped from there. It was while he had been in England that he had trained in the SOE and had come back to France in 1942 with the code name of Vladimir. Living above a tobacconist in Paris, he had let Yvonne know he was back. Building arms caches up pretty much by himself, and helping escaped POWs and downed pilots back to the UK, he had set up the Chestnut network and had recruited Uncle Robert and many others.

He then made me laugh telling me stories, such as the times he and Yvonne drove around Monaco in separate cars. He would lead and she would try and keep up as they raced around Monaco. Occasionally she would be stopped by the police for driving too fast. She would complain, "But I am only trying to keep up with my husband - why don't you stop him?"

They would come back and say, "We do not

stop the great Willy!"

The bruising in my shoulder was coming down now, and they suggested I should get a night's rest. Until they could or we could agree a plan, it was better I stay in the garage. I bedded down on a chaise longue in Robert's office. They laid blankets over me, and I drifted away feeling safe and warm.

The next morning they both came in with cheese and baguettes. We ate and Will looked at my shoulder. It was still sore and a little stiff, but the bruising had all but disappeared. Will produced another cream, saying this one would tighten the ligaments up in a few days. Then, and only then, they would help me move and get started.

The three of us discussed my future. They were very intent on my returning to England. I then told them about Albert and they both leant back in their chairs and whistled.

"You crazy girl, have you no idea how dangerous it is to be here? You cannot work with us, you know why. Now you tell us the truth; this is not a game. Those bastards out there play for real, do you understand?" said Robert.

I replied, "You have no idea how bloody hard it has been to get here. You have no bloody idea how easy I find it to kill, and you have no idea what I am prepared to do to get to him. With or without your help, I will play my part in this war - don't even try to stop me. Be with me if you choose, but I beg you not to be against me."

They retired for ten or fifteen minutes, returning with a compromise. Will spoke first. "Sweetheart it is with such a heavy heart we cannot allow you to work with us here. We understand your conviction, and know how stubborn you can be. So we have a suggestion that we think may work for you, and we can cope with."

I replied, "I'm listening!"

Willy then explained their plan and I took it all in. We went through how I would contact them; that I would be working alone. I must stay on the move to reduce the risk of capture. They would answer my coded letters through BBC broadcasts, confirming or refusing help with operations. They would courier money to me occasionally to prearranged drops, which we would work out there and then. Once this was all agreed they would get me out of Paris, with the correct clothing and passes to start my search!

As we all relaxed, knowing we had agreed a way to move forward, I asked, “Where is Jean-Pierre - why is he not here with you both?” Jean-Pierre Wimille had been Uncle Robert’s teammate and protégé, driving for Ettore Bugatti in the work’s Buggatis. Jean-Pierre had an accident before the war and was just making his comeback as it all got a little thick. He and Uncle Robert had won the Le Mans 24 Hours in 1937 and ’39. In 1933, Ettore Bugatti had invited him to become his official test driver. At that particular time, all they knew was that he had been designing cars for the public in the hope that he would be able to build them after the war. What they didn't know was that Jean-Pierre was also in the sabotage game!

Over the next few days we worked together on our future communication systems and codes. I was allowed to rest my shoulder. With the help of Willy's creams my ligaments tightened quickly and it was only three days before I had full movement and strength back. They had gone out and bought some beautiful clothes for me.

I laughed. "You bloody idiots! What the hell good are quality black market materials, never mind fancy coats and dresses?" They both looked at me, looking a little upset. Will spoke first, with his soft soothing tones.

"My little love, what have we done wrong for you? You are elegant, beautiful and you ooze style and confidence. Neither of us can ever see you in anything other than the most luxurious, designer clothing. We have burnt the clothing you arrived in. To Robert and I, it was not you."

"Oh shut up you two romantic idiots. Where

am I going to go to dinner parties? It's not like it was before this war. Some parts of your life may not have changed like they have for others. All I know is there will be no parties in the near future for me. I know you can't take the stuff back, but I also know my Aunts will take it, when you see them." I looked at them rather sternly I thought and then went on. "I need all the support I can get from you two. At the moment, sitting in the largest Bugatti dealership and garage in France, in the centre of Paris, is dangerous enough. I have no clothes as you have burnt what I had. You want to dress me like a doll and I am beginning to feel the need to thump one of you. What I do need is a country skirt or two, some cheap blouses, a couple of pairs of trousers for working in the fields, some working or walking style boots and a good rainproof coat. The girly stuff is out, do you two understand?"

Robert piped up and said, "I think we do - we were just so excited to see you and just got carried away. Once the people on the black market could see we were spending, they were not shy to take the opportunity to pile more onto us. We do understand and will put that right today. I can tell you that the navigator you sent back is in a bad way, but in the UK. He will be OK. He has asked for this message to be given to you. I quote: 'Hope never meet again, good luck'. I think you may have scared him a little."

I replied, "He's alive and at home; lucky, lucky boy."

Once we had my attire right and had sorted my papers and passes for my new role, we went through our goodbyes. This was harder than I thought; I had no idea how much I loved these two guys. They were just the best. Love oozed out of them - no wonder the crowds at the races and their fans loved them. They were just both unbelievably strong-willed, caring, gentle warriors of the track. I was taken by the cheeky buggers right up Avenue Foch and toward the Arc De Triomphe in a big

Bugatti; how they had the gall I will just never understand. They pointed out the SD and Gestapo Headquarters at numbers 84 and 85, and carried on through Paris. Before we were out of the true centre of Paris we stopped at a beautiful restaurant. We ate like royalty - the food was stupendous compared to the rations back in the UK. It was just fantastic.

Willy told me to memorise where we were, the name of the café and remember the head waiter was clean. He was not involved in the Resistance, but he was a safe friend with the ability to get to the two of them. I did as I was told and committed it to memory immediately.

We then travelled out on the hot, dusty roads past the outskirts of Paris and on. They were to drop me with a farmer who was safe. I was to stay at the farm for one night then get a move on. I still had intact the ninety thousand francs Vera at the SOE had supplied me with, so money was no problem, but as I had to carry it and it was cash, it could raise serious questions if found. Just another thing to be aware of!

After our goodbyes and the promise of seeing each other soon, they both left. My heart sank a little but the farmer and his wife were grand. Their dog, a beautiful black Labrador bitch, slept the night with me; it felt as if I were her responsibility. I have to say, I liked it!

Entry 4: Into the Unknown

I awoke with the cockerels the next morning, feeling pretty good. I went through all my kit again, just as had been done pre-flight by the SOE packers and then by the best two uncles one could ever have. My clothes were clean and were of local manufacture, with nothing that could give me away. My footwear was correct, with my city shoes in my bag. My papers I was assured were good. My pistol was in my pocket, a little spare ammunition in my handbag and I had cash in my suitcase. Now I had to go to my suggested starting point, going through Metz and then on to Strasbourg; I knew that Strasbourg was on the French-German border and Stuttgart was just a little further east where the Boch had their Mercedes-Benz factory. My two uncles had taken me as far as Chalons-en-Champagne, which was about halfway to my intended starting point. The farm I had stayed in overnight was far enough away from them not to cause either of us issues. I presumed they stayed somewhere else last night as they could not have got home before the curfew kicked in!

From here I made my way on to Metz and then back towards Luxembourg. The papers my uncles had provided were now becoming less and less effective. I just kept running the gauntlet across land, hoping to get to the Rhine; that had to be my best way up towards Switzerland and the area I was interested in. Uncle Robert and Uncle Willy had given me enough francs to add to the ninety thousand I had to bribe my way through most things as long as I kept my head, even though I still had to keep my head down and stay out of sight as best as I could. Whenever possible I would travel cross country by night, bathing in troughs and streams, keeping my clothing as clean as possible. Hotels could not be used but I did find the odd sympathetic farmer or two.

Eventually, after two weeks on my own, I reached the Rhine and then I fell lucky. I had skirted round Ettelbruck, Diekirch and Tandel in Luxembourg, avoiding contact with anybody and got to the Rhine. I really needed to bathe properly and after so long living off the land on the run, I was feeling pretty grimy.

I decided to take a risk; hiding all my clothes and the few things I had in the reeds on the river bank, I went for a swim. It was dusk, around 2230hrs. Going out a little too far, I became caught in the current. It was too much for me to combat and I started to drift downstream. Losing sight of my hiding place, I knew trouble was afoot. How the hell was I going to get back to my gear?

I then heard the rapid 'thonk' of a diesel and saw a rather large barge heading upstream towards me. It got closer and closer. The river was too wide and the surface too much like a looking glass to make a swim for it; the German guards or lookouts on her would see me instantly. The best I could hope was to ride her bow wave once she got close enough to me and escape to the shoreline that way.

As the barge got closer, I realised how big she was; not like a British sixty footer, she was more like a thirty thousand ton ship. Her beam had to be thirty to forty feet. I needed to swim hard or be hit! I started to stroke away like billy-o. This inevitably caused splashes and I was seen. There was no warning - high-speed lead just started to crack down towards me from the soldiers' rifles. A light came on and I was going nowhere in time. The barge was throttled back and started to slow down to next to nothing. I could do nothing but tread water until a line was hurled at me. I had no choice but to take it!

As I was drawn closer to the barge's side, the soldiers began to realise that I was a female in my birthday suit and dark haired, with matching collar and cuffs, so to speak. They started to josh each other as to their catch and who would have me for dinner!

At that point the Captain came out of the

bridge and started to have a go at the six German guards, stating that it was pretty unlikely that a slight girl with no clothes on would be too much of a threat to the mighty Third Reich. He offered to report them to their superiors and they reluctantly backed down. He and his mate hauled me in, took me on board and got me dried off.

About 0400hrs, Captain Jan Lever roused me in my bunk and asked if he could have a little chat. He spoke in French, as I had only communicated in French the night before. He wanted to know where I was from, why I had a Parisian accent and how it was that I had swum so far from my clothes. I went through this and gave the answers, knowing that telling the truth as far as possible made it much harder to spot a lie. My presumption was that the guards were listening through the air vents of the cabin.

The steel walls of the cabin were painted dark green. On the bulkheads, water was beading as the dew point fell in line with the ambient temperature. There were two bunks and a small table in the cabin. While we went through my story, I noticed his cap was partially on its side, over the back of the chair near the small table. I could just make it all out in the dim light. Captain Jan Lever was a stout chap, balding and portly, about five foot nine inches with a round face; probably liked a beer or two as his face was a little red, but that could be the outdoor life. His breath smelt of tobacco, but his smile was warm. His clothing was that of a Captain. His pullover was high necked, his trousers were moleskin and his unlit pipe hung from his unshaven jaw. His cap was black with gold braid - but inside the cap I could see a little glimmer of orange. My mind raced; could he be on our side, and if so, how the hell could I get him to give himself away? At least enough to get a little help!

As I talked away to him about needing a swim and getting caught in the current, thinking we must be miles upstream by now, I started to tap my finger on the bunk side. Slowly and gently, but very deliberately, I tapped the first verse of the Dutch National Anthem. Pausing, I then tapped out in Morse code the the Dutch King's name, then our King's name. I stopped to wait and hoped there would be some recognition. A tear slowly rolled away from his big, blue, left eye as he tried not to smile at me. He then leant forward and gave me a brief hug, whispering into my ear, "I understand. My crew and I are for you. We will find a way". He then left.

I was locked in the steel cabin. My life was now in the hands of Captain Jan Lever and his crew! Would I be questioned in the morning? Undoubtedly yes. Would I be turned over to the authorities or shot? There would little or no sleep for the rest of the night.

I can only presume dawn broke; all I could hear was the engine of the barge pounding away, spinning the propellor, thrusting us forward up the Rhine. I had no idea of the time until the second-in-command - I presume the engineer -came through the door with some pretty dire bread and a hot broth that tasted of nothing. But it was food and warmth! I still had a few rough blankets around me, and the crew had kept the Kraut guards away from me through the night. Things were looking up!

The man introduced himself as Johan Kendrew. As he handed the bread and broth to me, I reached forward with both hands, allowing my modesty to an extent to be exposed. He took his time but turned away slowly, after making an approving gesture with his lips. He then turned and took off his leather black cap, revealing a short back and sides haircut. A dirty neckerchief hung around his neck inside a grubby, collarless shirt. This was under a dark, leather waistcoat type of jacket. His sleeves were rolled up, baring forearms caked in grease and coal dust. He was broad across the back and his greasy trousers came up above his waist, and went down to a pair of clogs worn with no socks, showing ankles caked in dirt.

He spoke in Dutch at first I think, then used a little French. I responded to the French and he turned to me as I bade him. His right hand moved towards his buttons just below the rope that acted as a belt holding those trousers up. As he did this I readied myself as best I could for the forthcoming rape attempt. I only had two blankets and the empty broth mug to use against him, and was instantly ready in my crouched position on the bunk bed. He seemed to sense my response and lifted his left arm. As he did so, I leaped forward and took his middle fingers in the palm of my right hand. Stepping forward, I compressed the fingers in on themselves towards his palm. I lifted my left hand, allowing the mug to fall as my right leg came round behind his calves. He began to buckle backwards with the pain in his left hand, and fell over my right leg. I stepped around his back, placing my left forearm across his neck. Releasing his hand as he fell into me, I went onto my left knee, leaving the right one raised with the foot on the ground. My right hand now behind his head and the left hand cupping into my right elbow, his own body weight would break his neck if he struggled.

His hands dropped and he relaxed, then slowly his right hand rose up and I tightened my hold again. It moved slowly and deliberately towards the top of his trousers and then up a few inches to the same button as before on his pants. He turned the edge of his flies over, quite deliberately and slowly, revealing a tiny button sewn on the reverse side. It seemed to be a spare button. He rubbed it a little to reveal it was orange.

I immediately relaxed and helped him to his feet. He shook my hand and whispered, "We are for you! I will find some clothing. This morning early, our guards were changed. They know from the other guards there is a French girl we caught in the river yesterday. They will not touch you as long as they think we use you. Please you must strike and cut my face. This will keep the cover for you until we make a plan."

I smiled at him and let him leave with a loose tooth and a light graze just below his left eye - the same eye that would be black and very swollen shortly. The door was bolted behind him and I sat and waited again.

An hour or so later, Johan came back, this time with a German guard. The guard looked me up and down as Johan handed me some of his and Captain Jan's clothing. There were no shoes or clogs. The shirt I was given, I could get into twice, as with the heavy hessian pants that were very rough. The guard laughed at the state of me as I put these clothes on. Though I was dry, I must have looked like an orphan girl in grown ups' clothing. I think this allowed him to think I was about thirteen or so, rather than my true age. He left, shouting to his fellow guards that I was just a little child and to leave me to the crew for fun. I could be no danger to the Third Reich; there was no need to place me on the reports. Jo winked at me, then advised me that he would take the wheel and Captain Jan Lever would be with me soon. Again the door was closed behind him, only this time it was not bolted. I waited and waited.

Captain Jan Lever entered several hours later and advised me that the guards shift would be changed again shortly. He suggested that within a day or two the Krauts would not be aware I was there. He would somehow acquire some more suitable clothing and I was to become a crew member, cooking some of the rubbish they were all surviving on.

All went to this plan as we went further and further up the Rhine towards Switzerland. The trust between the three of us seemed to grow and after a few days we seemed to have gelled to an extent as a team. I needed to find a way to explain to Captain Jan that I needed to leave the vessel quietly and without being seen, somewhere around the French-Swiss border. He wanted to know why I did not want to sit out the war with them on the barge. Their chances of survival were good, the Allies were surely going to come this year and the bloody war would be over! I agreed that this would be a good plan, but still needed to give him a credible reason to disembark.

I told him I had grown up with the love of my life. He was a French pilot who had been flying from England. My stomach had always told me when he was on a mission and only settled when I thought he was safe again. A few days before they had fished me out of the Rhine, I had been really quite ill in the stomach. My mother had sat with me and asked if I was pregnant and instantly I went wild at her suggestion, telling her only Albert would ever be good enough. She knew how intuitive I could be, as her mother was the same.

After a long discussion, and after she had consulted with my grandmother, we felt that Albert must be in trouble – maybe shot down, injured or captured - but definitely not dead. With no communication with the UK or him, we were stumped as to what to do. My grandmother asked if I had a memento of Mr. Albert Noir and of course I said yes. I went to my room to find the one thing I had of his: a red neckerchief he had always worn before he joined the French Air Force. She instructed me to bring it.

She took a pencil from her bag and and tied a thread to it. Then on some scraps of paper she drew some fan shapes. These fan shapes were divided into quarters. On each quarter, words were written: Injured, Captured, Running, Dead. The next one read France, Germany, Switzerland, Holland. The next, North, South, East, West. These fans added up to about seven or eight in total. She took them one by one and held the pencil up by the thread. At the centre bottom of the drawn fan shape she placed the edge of Albert's neckerchieif under her forefinger. She then seemed to focus her mind and drift a little. Her right hand was steady as a rock, but even so the pencil started to swing. As it did so, it would go to and fro over one part of the fan shape and one word. Each time she would write the word down that the pencil had been swinging over, then repeat the exercise over the next drawn fan shape. At the end she read out loud to my mother and me the following: alive, injured, running. Northeast French-Swiss border. Not Safe!

My mother, I told him, turned to me and looked me in the eye. She told me that my gran had the gift; she had never been wrong when she did this. My stomach problem was a similar thing, to do with empathy for another and being in tune. If I was willing to risk my life to find him, she would not stand in my way, but she knew of no way to help me!

"That night I left and now, here I am!"

Captain Jan Lever whistled lightly at me from across the Bridge, and looked me up and down as he held the wheel. He said, "My mother had the gift. In two days we will be at a good starting point for you. The river turns and we get very close to the bank side, where if no rain comes it will be dry. We will distract the guards and you must jump. We can cover for you and they will lose the fact you have gone over the side in a day or two, as they change shifts. We can do nothing else to help but pray for you."

I replied, "That is enough; I can do the rest!"

He then came back to me very quietly and almost whispered, "I think I know where you learnt to fight, as Jo has described it to me. You had me going with your gran as my mother does do this. If there is anything you want, I don't have it, but I do know a few people in the area you may want to make contact with.

Sure enough, two days later Captain Jan took me to one side again and said to me, "Regarding footwear and a few other things. I have let you down - but you have children's feet, what could I do? Everything else you need you have. I am going to set up planks to either side of the vessel and run some fishing lines off them. The Boche will think we are hoping to have fish for dinner and will do nothing after a short while.

'At dusk I need you to be ready; as the river for us comes from the starboard side, I will guide the vessel to that shoreline. I will hit her hull on the sandbank and then throttle up to push the bow forward, while swinging the wheel to port. This will push the stern into the shore. You will have five or so senconds to make your jump from the plank onto the shore. I will then have to spin the wheel to starboard to get her round the bend in the river. You should make the reeds easily enough but you must keep you head down. The two names of farms I have given you will help but if you can avoid asking it would be better. Be ready little lady, just be ready and oh yes, good luck!"

The little gear they had sorted for me I was either wearing, or it was in my pockets. All went to plan and I took a running leap, twenty feet out with a ten foot drop into the reeds. I waited for the barge to disappear into the distance. No alarms were sounded so that looked good to me; off again on my mission.

As it was dusk and I was to some extent in the country, I could move with relative ease and speed. I soon found the first farm Captain Jan had mentioned. Rather than approach anybody, I searched and stole what I could and kept moving. I presumed they had a teenage daughter and son as their clothes were almost dry on the washing line. Between them I was quickly dressed in fitting clothes with a pair of boots that fitted too. Oh happy days!

I moved on to the next farm by 0400hrs and hunted round for some things I could use as weapons. I acquired a little sock darning tool, a knife and a pistol with a little ammunition. Hopefully the farmer would not miss them until I was long gone. Then I was off, heading further upriver and wondering how I was going to acquire some money, as it would be hard enough without papers, never mind having nothing to bribe people with. This meant getting to a lightly populated area, pickpocketing a few strangers and doing a touch of breaking and entering; not the sort of thing I would normally choose to do. After the war they all were compensated through the post with a letter explaining my needs at the time.

Entry 5: Acts of Sabotage – and Discovery

Robert, through the Bugatti dealership, had a freedom few people enjoyed from the Germans. He would get permits to travel under the guise of servicing or repairing vehicles and was able to travel over large parts of France. The Resistance, through Robert, was able to use the vehicles to pick up arms from air drops by the British. Robert and Willy were creating stockpiles of arms and munitions ready for the Allied invasion and they worked relentlessly to recruit partisans for Resistance work. Their aim was to create as much disruption to the German war machine as possible, then to assist the Allies when France and Paris were to be liberated.

While my uncles carried on their work, I did as we had agreed: to work at putting together Resistance teams, train them and get them operational. This I did, but never staying with the cell I created too long as I had to find Albert.

Eventually and quite by accident I found two guys who became the mainstay of my team. These were Erich Krahenbuhl, a Swiss, and Stuart Latimer, an Irishman. I bumped into them when I was looking over a potential target on the Rhine near the Swiss border. I watched them go into a river harbour, bold as you like, get onto barges, move around a bit and then get off. At the time I thought they must be to do with German security as they moved with such ease. They then disappeared into the ether and I tried to follow them through my binoculars. Just as I was losing them there were two bloody large explosions. The barges they had been on went up in flames with their cargoes of fuel. I had to find these guys.

I could not go into the town as I had no cover story to be there and so went to the mountainside to overview the main roads out of the town. An hour later I saw them, happy and carefree as you like, making their way into the tree line. Nobody chasing them, they just strolled and laughed. I made my way along, keeping an eye on them from a thousand yards away. They then got on horses and started riding up the mountainside towards me. I had a few grenades as well as my pistol by now, but that was my full compliment of weapons - plus my knife and the little wooden darning tool.

I skirted round, trying to get in line with the direction they seemed to be following. As they drew closer, I could hear them laughing and joking, still in French. As they approached, they slowed and seemed to be instinctively wary. I knew with my training from Kevin that there was no way I had left any indications of my movements. It could be they - or the horses - had sensed me. Jumping out, gun in hand I requested them to alight from their horses and explain what I had witnessed. They did so calmly, while assessing their surroundings and myself. They could see I was by myself with no back-up so they went to jump me. The gun was knocked out of my hand and away. They drew knives and really had a good go. I don't really think they were trying to kill me, although later they swore they were. The fight only lasted a few minutes and once they were both laid out unconscious I waited for the first to stir.

The shorter one stirred first, moaned and then said in English with an Irish accent, "Bejesus, what the fook happened?" I sat there and laughed as he started to try and move. He then realised his pants were down around his ankles and his hands were tied to his friend's hands above his head, with one of their sets of braces. The belt the other one had used to keep his pants up was tightened around their necks, holding their heads together back-to-back. He struggled and found it not possible to get free as I had also tied their trouser legs together. He then said, after he realised his head really hurt, "What the hell are you, a bloody one woman army?"

I laughed. I knew I could get on with this Irish fool. He had guts and nerve; he would just need some training and maybe to learn to fight a lot better than he had. He was around five foot eight inches tall when standing, had a tanned unshaven face, hair thinning slightly and bleached by the sun. He had sparkling blue eyes that would seem to be full of mischief. I told him that I was known as Murtyl, nothing else, and he told his name was Stuart Latimer.

At this point the harder one started to stir. I would say he was harder, only because his fighting was much more controlled, with structure and purpose to his attempted blows. It was later that I explained how a humble wooden sock-darning dolly had been used to render then both unconscious. Using it like a kosh, a little tap just at the base of the skull behind the ear worked a treat. This one had the same struggle but soon realised he was not going anywhere until I knew what I wanted to know. So he introduced himself as Erich, a Swiss from Stafa near Lake Zurich. A few years older than Stuart, he was smaller in height, maybe five foot four, and was a similar build to Kevin Mooney. Obviously well-accomplished with horses, he had brown eyes and dark hair with a weathered look. He was an ex-Swiss army chef who wanted to fight. His country was neutral and by the time he was ready, there was only England to join up with, and he stood no chance of getting there to do so. So he came over to Montreux, hoping to find a way to do some good. He had met Stuart who was working for Charlie Chaplin doing some gardening and general house duties, helping in the vineyards and wine presses, and acting as a general gopher (going for this and going for that). Charlie, officially sitting out the war, had been accused of all sorts of shit by the American studios after the First World War. This time, although too old to get involved much, he was doing a few things on the quiet; he was financing these two. Officially they worked around the property, but Charlie would help plan some of their clandestine work. He helped them improve basic formulae to make explosives and to go into the mountains to assess the power of them. Once they got a good formula, the two would drift off on horse back cross country, find the target Charlie had chosen, then find a way to take it out. They would then go back to Charlie's and carry on. It tickled Charlie to read in the newspaper that the Germans could never understand how with no air or commando raids etc. they could be attacked so far behind the front line.

That had been some information to take in, but if these guys could get in and out of Switzerland without detection they had to be worth knowing. Risky I know, but my instincts allowed me to go with the flow. I never regretted this. They took me to Montreux and I stayed with them at Charlie's place. I trained them in combat. They produced explosives, which we moulded into all sorts of shapes, from potatoes to vermin.

Together we went out on two missions and developed a formula. I would write in code to Willy and Robert about a target we thought we could take, such as a railway terminal and yard. When we got the go-ahead via the BBC World Service in code and a date for a local air raid in that area, we would be off. The idea was to get into the area with a couple of weeks leeway. Erich and Stuart would dig in and hide out with a view of our target. I would get a job in a local bar to fraternise with the locals, while looking for potential Resistance people to assist. I would befriend a high-ranking German officer. This would be achieved by the following route: borrowing, stealing or acquiring, by some method or other, some rather risqué clothing. This would be a white blouse, as close-fitting as I could manage, using the buttons only up to a point where privacy of my anatomy was just kept; the collar would be up and my hair down just over my shoulders. Then a black skirt, tight fitting to around my knees - you may call it a pencil skirt - with a cut from the hem in line with the outside of my right leg. This cut would go up two-thirds revealing, when sitting down, a rather large portion of my thigh. The lads did think it was a bit raunchy, and it did get those officers excited shall we say.

My next step took the whole exercise a little deeper. If a cheroot was available I would smoke one; not great but it was fashionable then. More interestingly for the Bosch officer was to see me drinking. I would order a champagne flute and get the barman to fill it with a light, local French beer, betting the barman I could drive the Nazi officer mad just with one drink. As you might guess, they would see the new girl in town, which would be interesting enough, but to see her alone and drinking, while dressed as I was, meant they would not leave me alone (which was the idea).

They would ask if I was alone; I would reply yes. Then could they buy me a drink? The answer would be, of course but on a few conditions: 1: they should expect nothing in return. 2: they could only buy me the drink I was drinking. 3: they had to guess what it was. 4: they could not touch my glass. 5: they could not smell my glass and 6: they could not ask the barman, who was sworn to secrecy.

They would look at the colour and see the bubbles. They instantly thought it was champagne with a mixer. As they ran through many ideas, they would try and tempt me with champagnes and other drinks at all sorts of prices. The bar put the prices up as they bought more and more. Once a bottle was opened, the fools just drank, never learning what the barman and I had arranged. This made it incredibly easy to pick out a strategic target, and who the superiors were, not only by rank, then use the knowledge against them. It worked a treat on all our raids in one form or another as we moved from location to location.

Then on the night of the planned raid, I would be particularly friendly. The aim was to be invited back to the barracks and get into their quarters - allow the chosen ranking officer to drink a little more than the last few evenings, and let him get physically close to me. Once partially dressed, and allowing the officer to feel he was in control, I would tease him into a fun fight. This was then used as an opportunity to clip his wings and render him unconscious, restrain and gag him. If this could not be achieved quickly, a sharpened knitting needle, slipped out of my handbag, would be thrust into his heart through his tunic, to the left hand side of his back between the fourth and fifth rib, directly through the pericardium and into the heart.There would be no coming back from that!

By the time those who were allowed to live came round, I would be dressed in my blacks. My skirt and blouse would be burning in the fireplace and my incendiary devices would be hanging from my belt. It was my job then to set the timed incendiary devices all around the barracks. The small amount of high explosives we could get near the camp would be lobbed in by the lads at pre-arranged points near targets. These I would then place and set, then I would aim to get off-campus.

The three of us, and any others we had been able to recruit, would then spread out around the outside of the campus perimeter and wait.

Once the devices started to go off, the solders would run to their action stations while looking for intruders. The incendiaries would ignite, releasing their extraordinary heat and flame, setting the target ablaze.

We would shoot as many of the soldiers as possible in a hail of highspeed lead when they appeared out of their barracks, allowing the bodies to pile up one on another. Then we would retreat. The RAF bombers, if on time and close by, could see from fifty or sixty miles away the target being attacked due to the light of the flames against the blacked-out suroundings. Their raids were successful, partly because we had destroyed the German ground-to-air defence, allowing the aircraft more time to sight their targets.

On one particular raid Erich, Stuart and I were a little late retiring from the objective - or it could have been that the RAF boys above were just a little early. Either way, I caught a blow from the blast from one of the charges they had dropped and got thrown into a boulder, striking my right femur which was cleanly broken into two parts rather than the preferred one-part version. We were potentially buggered. The lads quickly splinted my leg and we got as far away as we could from the target. Once dawn arrived we needed to re-assess the situation and formulate a new exit plan, then separate.

It was unlikely I could do the three or four days back to Montreux. Public transport, trains etc. would be under high security and a woman with a broken leg would attract a lot of attention. So we sat and thought about it.

Erich came up with a plan. We were within twenty five miles or so from Dole in northeastern France. He knew of a monastery where I might be able to get help, or at least find sanctuary. We fiddled our way to the outskirts of Dole. Erich, bless him, seemed to know his way around and got us in, in one go - straight to the monastery he wanted to go to! We missed various checkpoints and once in the grounds Stuart stayed with me while Erich approached and then knocked on the door. He was able to get a little time with a monk, who said that although he would like to help they were always being watched by the Germans and continuously checked by them.

However once he saw the state I was in, he suggested we wait. A few hours later we met Charles for the first time. He appeared out of the dark and asked us to follow, letting us know he was a monk who came from another part of the Dole Monastery. The Nazis had never found his group of buildings due to its location and the way the river flowed through the forest and around the town.

He took us to a crypt and examined me. There was no infection, which was good. Using herbs, acupuncture and homeopathy he calculated I would be up and moving in under three weeks.

Erich and Stuart had to return to Montreux and so left me under the care of Charles.

Over the next few days we became friends, even though I was a little grumpy, impatient and downright annoying as his patient. It went as follows: I was placed on a bed where he could bathe me regularly and I could be kept comfortable. My ablutions were to be made possible through a hole in the structure.

The first few days there I was in light traction; this was achieved using a weight off the end of the bed structure, connected to a rope which was tied to some straps placed around the ankle of the injured leg. Twice each day he rubbed oil containing arnica, rhus toxicodendron and symphytom officinale into my leg, which he said would reduce the bruising and swelling very quickly. It did do this very quickly!

Once the swelling had subsided, he splinted my femur and braced it so that I could not move it while sleeping. To accelerate the healing process he performed the weirdest thing I had ever seen done: inserting two acupuncture needles in my upper thigh, one in a spot he named as Bi Guan (Stomach 31) and the other in a spot he named Liangqui (Stomach 34), he rotated each of the needles by rotating them individually in a clockwise action.

After this he took a piece of insulated wire and attached one end of the wire by crocodile clip to one needle and the other end to the other needle. He then explained that for a bone to heal naturally, several things must be in place: treatment must start within six weeks of the original accident, or that would have to be re-initiated by another action (I did not have to worry about that). The bones should be set and in our case we could only use light traction and splint or support, as he had nothing to set the leg with. The oils had been used as I have told you. He told me that the acupuncture should do the following: the body communicates cell-to-cell through chemicals produced by organs and by electricity produced by the cells. This electricity ran usually at between three and five ohms. In order for the bone to heal as quickly as possible he had created a circuit around the break, so for the body to complete the circuit it would allow one of the broken ends to act as cathode and the other end to work as an anode. This would mean one end of the bone would dissolve slowly and the other end would receive these calcium ions. This would quickly allow a bridge to develop between the two broken ends of the bone. He then asked me if I could feel anything. I answered that there was a tickle or a trickling feeling where the break was.

He laughed and said, "Well young lady you can feel it working."

I laughed too, and said, "You're joking, how long will it take to become strong?"

His reply was quite startling. "If you agree to allow it to heal properly and eat as I instruct, we will get plenty of calcium and so on into you. Then you should be walking in ten days and looking to start training lightly with me in fifteen or so."

I replied, "Surely that's not right - this is a six week plus thing at home!"

"Yes," was the reply. "It is for allopathic medicine and in the modern medical world, but in my world of traditional medicine from China and Tibet, these things are possible. How many Chinese and Tibetans do you see walking around with plasters on and using crutches?" I had no answer to this as I had never met a person from that part of the world.

Over the next ten days, he repeated the exercise a few times and turned me over to do the same on the Urinary Bladder Meridian on the back of the injured leg. Sure enough, I was walking fairly comfortably in ten days.

He explained a little about his history and where he had learned this form of medicine and why. He also explained that his skills allowed him to physically take a body from a state of Diss-ease to a state of Ease, allowing it to heal itself much more rapidly - which is where the other skills came into effect. He then went on to teach me, in an attempt to keep my mind occupied, how the Chinese Five Elemental system worked - a little about herbs, and that essential oils are fantastic tools but you have to understand that they act like hormones; as such they can directly affect the central nervous system and must be treated with great respect. Every patient should be typed according to the Chinese Five Elemental system prior to using them.

I found the things he was teaching me intriguing and it seemed to make a great deal of sense. He also would sit and meditate quite close to me. The first time he did this, I asked when he finished - or at least seemed to become awake again - what he had been doing.

He replied, "Stepping out, feeling and conveying my electromagnetic energy towards your broken femur to assist the healing."

"No, that cannot be you making the rough

ends of my femur feel itchy and hot!" I instantly replied.

He smiled, rubbed his hands together while breathing deeply, and placed his open hands, palms facing, about four inches above my body. He then said, "I will focus my mind and visualise the centre of one palm spinning clockwise and the other spinning anti-clockwise. Please let me know what you find." Quickly I felt I a pushing effect and heat from his right hand and a cool, pulling effect from his left. I told him and he instantly reversed the rotations in his mind. The feeling changed and reversed on my body!

He then went onto explain that nature's way of sedating was to move in an anti-clockwise direction, and to stimulate, to rotate things clockwise. He had decided that if I was willing to learn he would teach me for as long as I chose to learn. He believed from the few days he had known me that I had empathy for this. I explained about my gran and he laughed. "Yeehhs I know. As you have become stronger I have been able to feel your presence. You show no natural aggression but are decisive and willing to take immediate action according to the situation. That is ideal for what I will teach you. Whatever business you are in, it will stand you in good stead by creating a greater balance and sensitivity within you!"

Then he went on with the meditation and how to increase my awareness of myself and the environment around; how to still myself properly, learning and listening more acutely than I had ever done or experienced before. It fitted in so well with my SOE work. I was quite astonished that this would only allow me to become a better agent than my superiors could have hoped! We then started to practise martial arts to build my stamina back up and I was surprised at how adept Charles was as an opponent and training partner.

A few days before the boys returned, Charles told me about a patient he had in his charge. He could not send him back to the UK, as he did not have the contacts. The abbot knew nothing about his past, or that Charles was helping persons such as me and downed RAF boys, as well as POW escapees. If he was able to help them recover from injury, all he could do then was turn them out, as he had no contact with the outside world, never mind the Resistance. This was a dilemma for him and he asked if we could help. I explained the mission I was officially on, but not my personal agenda.

He then told me he had a French pilot in another part of the crypt. He had sustained a head injury and Charles was struggling with it all. All physical injuries had healed well, but the bang on the head seemed to have created some emotional problems. Maybe I could meet this guy and at least give a view from a different angle. I thought why the hell not? I had a few days to go before the lads would be back.

As Charlie took me by the hand to lead me to the area where this chap was hiding, my stomach started to churn. Then I heard the whistle, and my knees buckled.

As I fell, I turned to Charles and said, "You have the man I'm looking for – Albert - don't you?"

Charles, astonished, looked at me and said, "How the hell do you know who he is?"

I replied, "He is the reason I am here!" I got to my feet and ran forward to see Albert.

On entry to the darkly lit room I saw him, one hand on a mug of something, whistling, while he sketched something with the other hand. He turned and looked up at me. He obviously recognised me, but that emotion, that sparkle, the glint in his eye was just not there! He stood up and walked over to me, shook my hand, and welcomed me.

As time passed over the next few days, I found the connection was still there. He trained with Charles and me. Our ability to read each other's thoughts was there and Charles was mesmerised. Everything was there except that ability to feel that one emotion. It broke my heart!

The lads returned and between us we explained to Albert what we were doing from Montreux in front of Charles. Immediately Albert was in on the action and Charles suggested we use him where we could. As we got to know Charles better he became an essential part of my team through the years.

Entry 6: to Paris

We started to use Dole as a store, staging post and hideout. We carried out several more missions without mishap following the protocol originally set up with Uncle Willy and Robert. Then it happened.

My action plan card had gone off to my heroic Grand Prix uncles and I waited to get confirmation from the BBC that our raid was approved. No approval came and I listened for several nights to the BBC. Eventually a coded message was read out with my contact poem, at the correct time. It was not confirmation of going into action again but a plea. It took a while to decode, as I had to re-read it several times to believe it. Essentially it stated, "Chestnut broken, high-ranking members captured by the Gestapo in Paris. Help or neutralise where possible." This was around July 14th, 1944.

To me this meant at least Uncle Willy and Uncle Robert were captured; if not already they would soon be tortured for information. To either kill them or effect their escape was the request from England. I spoke to the lads and explained the history and what it all meant to me. Without hesitation they all volunteered to help me, and go to Paris.

We would have to travel in pairs, as a group of four would cause suspicion. If possible we would find help or at least get some local information. It was in no way a low risk strategy, but we were on the move within twelve hours of the notification. I had no way of communicating with England, so we had to go blind, with no contacts. We would be hunted by the Gestapo, the SD the SS and by the Resistance. Everything we had done before had been supported in some way or another. Although at present Robert and Willy were probably on a one-way ticket, this essentially could have been for us too.

Albert and I took the train to Reims and then on to Paris. We had no in-date forged papers and were going to have to dodge the authorities all the way. Erich and Stuart were travelling by road; the same applied to them. Our aim was to meet three hundred yards west of the west wing of Notre-Dame Cathedral in two days at noon; find our way into the catacombs and try to pick up some local assistance there.

How we made it I'll never really know. Once, on a train, a lady had been holding her baby for hours. She was obviously hungry and tired. Just as two men in black leather trenchcoats came into our car, I offered to hold the sleeping baby to give the woman some rest. Papers were asked for. Albert moved and went between the carriages and somehow hid under the train. I held the baby, and, as the men approached asking for papers, the child's mother got hers out for inspection. I fumbled around towards my pockets and shushed the men, asking them to come back in a few minutes, while I fiddled the papers out without waking the child. They got to the end of the crowded carriage and turned, looking back at me. I waved a card above my head at them and they made a hand signal which I can only assume meant OK, we can't be bothered to come back up the carriage to look.

After a short while I passed the child back to its mother. The woman looked at me quizzically, then shrugged and went on minding her own business.

Albert and I had agreed to jump a few miles prior to Paris in the countryside to avoid the authorities at the station. Through good judgment and a lot of luck we got into Paris and into the catacombs, close to the Arc de Triomphe, and waited.

I asked Albert to stay put, and went to our rendezvous and caught up with Erich and Stuart. We quickly headed back to Albert's hiding place, very close to Avenue Foch, in the catacombs.

Through reputation and before I had left England, I knew that the SD, SS and Gestapo headquarters were somewhere very near. Then I remembered my bold uncles pointing out the buildings on Avenue Foch on the last day I had seen them; we needed to find out which building our targets would be in, watch it and make plans, then make an attempt to get them out.

It turned out that a few of the Resistance were using the catacombs as a hideout and to move around the city. One, named Christophe, a short, rotund chap, with thick spectacles and an ever-smiling face, balding head and as scruffy as they come, settled us in. He had been using the catacombs pretty much as soon as Paris was occupied. He had been showing the Resistance, whenever he could, how to move around the city with least danger of capture. He had exceptional knowledge and soon brought us up to speed with who had been captured and where they were being held. It turned out that the German counterintelligence branch of the SS, known as Sichereitsdienst, or the SD, used numbers 82, 84 and 86, Avenue Foch.

Number 84 was used specifically for the imprisonment and torture of captured SOE agents in France. There seemed to be frequent transfers of these prisoners from number 84 to Fresnes Prison, on the outskirts of Paris. The second floor housed the SD's wireless section controlled by Joseph Goetz, from where the radio games with the SOE were conducted, using captured wireless sets and codes from captured code books. This meant nothing to me, as I had no transmitter since my arrival in France.

The fourth floor was taken up as the offices and private quarters of Sturmbannführer Josef Kieffer, who was in charge of number 84. On the fifth (top) floor were the guardrooms, an interpreter's office and cells for the confinement of prisoners under interrogation.

It was at this point that Christophe was able

to tell us that Uncle Willy had actually been captured earlier in 1943 and it would seem he had held out through all his interrogators' actions, then been taken to Berlin for further questioning. He was unable to tell me too much about Uncle Willy's capture, but was able to confirm he had never divulged any information. In four months in Avenue Foch they had not broken him. Vogt and his entourage had eventually deported him to Berlin for even more hell. He was sorry that nothing had been done to help him be freed; he just hoped that Willy Grover-Williams, the brave-hearted racing driver, was still alive.

At around 0930hrs, a number of German vehicles had arrived at Willy's home near Auffargis. There were around fifteen German officers in plain clothes, under the command of Karl Langer - a typical SS officer in a black, long, leather coat, strutting around shouting orders. They went straight for Willy. Langer was not subtle, and as his men searched the house, Willy was captured.

Langer ordered a Spaniard called Señor Jean to soften the prisoner up. The SD often used foreigners to do their dirty work against suspected SOE agents. This even included a traitor called Harold Cole, an Englishman.

Will had given nothing away, but Will's parents and family were there and they were questioned too. The younger ones had known nothing, and then Señor Jean was instructed to attack Willy's parents George and Jeanne Grover, demanding to know where the arms dumps were.

While this was happening, Maurice Benoist arrived at Auffargis with Vogt and a guy called Peters who was working for the SD. Peters' real name was Pierre Cartaud; he knew all about the British-backed French Resistance, simply because until his arrest in May 1942 he had been a part of it. Code-named Capri, he acted as a courier for Colonel Remy's intelligence in Bordeaux, supplying information to the British about German movements. After his arrest he worked for the

Nazis and the information he gave them led to the arrest of hundreds in Remy's network. From there Peters put everything into catching British agents. After a year he had the Nazis' full confidence. George Grover lasted eight hours or so of interrogation before he relented and told them the little he did know. It was enough for the Germans to start a detailed search of the outbuildings. After originally only finding three revolvers, the search produced fifty one canisters full of weapons in an old well and forty seven more behind a false wall in the stable block, with a dozen parachutes.

Maurice and Willy were taken back to the fifth floor at Avenue Foch by Vogt and Peters. Maurice was freed quite quickly, which led Willy to become suspicious of Maurice's allegiances.

Willy was able to get a message to his wife Yvonne. It read: "There is little hope and you must get out of Paris". She hid for the next three weeks at a friend's house in Thorens, just north of Grasse.

At 1930hrs Willy's interrogation was started

by Vogt and lasted all night. It was not believed that Willy had talked but they seemed to know all about Chestnut and were after Robert Benoist, steadily intensifying the search. They knew they had a high-ranking SOE man, or at least he must be high up in the Resistance after finding the arms dumps.

Entry 7: Robert Benoist's Story

Robert went to ground as Paris was becoming too dangerous for him to operate any longer. He stayed low for a day or so but soon felt he needed to know what was going on, at least with his father and mother. He did not make contact with any of his Resistance group, as he knew they were probably being watched. So he found a post office that did not seem to be under surveillance and used the telephone, knowing all calls went through switchboards and it would take a few moments to be put through. All he needed to hear was one of his parents' voices to know they had not been taken prisoner, and then he could hang up and go. He made his call and waited; it was taking a lot longer than usual and after forty or so seconds he decided to leave without being connected. He left the post office, realising that the operator on the exchange had a strong German accent and his parents' telephone number was probably under surveillance.

As he left the post office in the Place Gambetta, he could not know the operator had already reported to the SD at Avenue Foch that an unknown was calling from Place Gambatta post office to Robert Benoist's parents' telephone number. The Germans thought it could be Robert and sent a car.

Robert was walking briskly down the street when a man approached him from behind and said, "Bonjour, Monsieur Benoist." Robert realised that although the man had spoken in French, his accent was just not quite right! So he ignored it. It was said again and the man was so close now that Robert could not ignore it. He turned and looked blankly at the person, hoping to bluff his way through the danger by saying it must be a case of mistaken identity. The man continued to speak and Robert realised there were several men approaching from different directions.

A car pulled up and it was too late, he was

bundled into the back of a car. There was no escape; there were four of them in the car. He protested, but his captors ignored him and drove him towards Avenue Foch. One drove, one was in the passenger seat and two were in the back with him. Robert placed his hands on the back of the seats either side of them, to give his shoulders more room. As the vehicle sped towards Avenue Foch it rolled quite heavily while travelling round the corners. He also realised that the design of the car meant that the leather straps along the inside of the door acted as opening devices. He grabbed hold of them on both sides and waited. His captors did not notice.

If they were to take the logical route to Avenue Foch, they would pass by the large department stores behind the opera House and continue up Boulevard Haussmann until they got to the Arc de Triomphe. From there it would be just a few hundred meters to the SD headquarters. He worried there would be no other opportunity to make a break, but the driver then took an unexpected turn at the junction of Rue de Richelieu, probably heading for the Ministry of Interior where the Gestapo had offices.

Taking the opportunity as the car swung right, he lurched himself at the German next to him while releasing the door. The German rolled out of the car with Robert close behind; he used the German to break his fall.

In an instant he was on his feet and running. The car had skidded to a halt and there was confusion behind. He ran, ducking and diving between pedestrians. By the time the Germans were aware Robert was not lying in the road with their colleague, Robert had already gone.

Robert went into the arcade Passage de Princes and cut through from Rue de Richelieu to the Boulevard des Italians. Here people surrounded him, so he quietly made his way through Boulevard Haussmann and assessed the damage to his clothes. He knew he looked out of place with the tears in his clothing and needed to change. He headed down L'avenue Hoche to try and find his old friend from World War One, pilot and racer, Roger Labric who had an apartment next to Salle Pleyel concert hall. From there at least he could make a call to a faithful employee at the Bugatti garage and get someone he trusted to get him some new clothes, and then make his way to a car he had hidden.

His employee L'Antoine answered his call. Robert spoke first. "This is Robert," he said before L'Antoine could speak. "Meet me at 16 Avenue Hoche."

There was a pause. "You mean at Bugatti's?" L'Antoine asked.

"Yes," Robert replied and rang off, worried that if he stayed on the line too long the call would be traced.

What Robert did not know, was that when L'Antoine had answered the telephone he was surrounded by four Germans. Two were in uniform carrying machine guns and two in plain clothes. They had burst into the room only moments before, demanding to know where Robert Benoist was. They threatened to take L'Antoine and his wife to prison if he did not cooperate. He had no idea what had happened or where Robert was.

Then the telephone had rung! The two plain clothes Germans had heard everything; they demanded L'Antoine drive them immediately in Benoist's car to Avenue Hoche. His wife would be held captive by the uniformed soldiers to guarantee compliance.

What only L'Antoine knew was that in Robert's rush he had made a mistake when he had said the Bugatti offices were at 16 Avenue Hoche. In fact there was nobody in the building called Bugatti; Ettore Bugatti's apartment and drawing office were several hundred meters further up Avenue Hoche. L'Antoine dropped the two Germans off at number 16 and they went to find the Bugatti apartment.

They were confused by the answers they got, which amounted to the fact that nobody called Bugatti lived in the building. The Germans were not quite sure what to do, but they had heard the conversation so they would wait in the car outside, hoping Robert would emerge from hiding.

Robert was unable to see what was going on below from Labric's apartment. He decided to call the Bugatti office and talk to Ettore's secretary, Georges Clavel - a man he knew he could trust. He asked Clavel to see if his car was waiting outside. Clavel went outside to look, then returned to tell Robert it was standing several hundred meters further down the road. L'Antoine was in it, but there were also two other men sitting in the back seats. He thought it may be a trap and to find another way out of the building.

Labric's apartment was on the top floor with access to the roof. Robert decided to sit it out on the roof, with Labric in the apartment; if it was searched there should be no reason to go on the roof since Labric was there. As he went up the air raid sirens began to sound. Everybody was heading for the air raid shelters and Robert knew he could not risk being caught in one. Labric latched the skylight and left Robert on the roof.

Once it was dark and Labric had not returned, Robert made his way across the roofs to Salle Pleyel next door. He broke in through a skylight and left a message to say he would pay for the damage he had caused. He then made his way to the ground floor and was challenged by the night watchmen. They had a little banter and a drink then Robert asked if the night watchmen would check there were no Germans on the street. He was given the all clear and left.

Knowing the midnight curfew was coming soon he did not risk trying to get across the city. He could not go to any of his known friends so he made his way to a family he had met once or twice. He asked Monsieur Dupuy if he could put him up for the night as he had been caught out by the curfew. Monsieur Dupuy and his family agreed, as they had no knowledge of Robert's activities. He left before the family awakened so as not to place them in danger.

The Germans asked Charles Escoffier if the car he stored there was Robert Benoist's. When Robert went to a local café and telephoned le Grand Garage de la place Clichy in the Rue Forest, he was told the Germans had taken it!

Robert then waited for office hours and telephoned the Bugatti showroom on the L'avenue Montaigne and spoke to his secretary, Stella Tayssadre. She knew from Clavel that Robert was on the run from the Germans and she took no persuasion to offer to help him. They arranged to meet and she took him to her family's apartment, 67 Boulevard Poniatowski, in the southeast of Paris. She then returned to work promising she would come back with updates on what was happening

The next day - a Saturday - Robert decided

to try again to make contact with Henri Dericourt. He went to their usual rendezvous at the Ping Pong Bar in La Rue Brunel, just off the Avenue de la Grande Armée. He told the SOE Air Movement Officer what had happened and that he must get out of France as soon as possible. Henri agreed and assured Robert that he would find space for him on one of his secret flights to the UK. Henri said that he would telephone Stella at the Bugatti garage when all was arranged, using the passphrase 'Do you have news of Maurice?'

For twelve days Stella was Robert's eyes and ears. She passed everything on she heard in the Bugatti offices and made contact with several survivors of networks for him. There could be no flight out until later in August, because the moon would be too bright. He had to wait; there were too many paper checks on the streets so he had to stay in the apartment.

Robert Benoist was actually only second on Henri Dericourt's list of priorities. Nick Boddington had been flown in, to independently assess the damage to the networks from England. The Germans knew he was there and were intent on finding him. Henri had to insist on Nick hiding outside of Paris in the country. When the moon was favourable, and Henri had got Nick out by Lysander from near Tours, he then allowed his priorities to roll round to others in trouble. He actually had eight agents who desperately needed to get out of France and back to England. This was way too many for a Lysander to be used; they used a Lockheed Hudson once Henri had located a suitable landing area.

The flight Robert was on, got ten SOE agents out from all over France. It was a very daring pick up - or stupid, looking at the list of SOE operatives' names.

Once landed in England they were all taken to the Royal Victoria Patriotic School in the middle of Wandsworth Common. It was not a very welcoming building and Robert felt it was like a prison. It gave the British time to go through everybody's stories.

Once they had been picked through, one of the returned SOE agents was proved to have become a double agent. Though they still went through all of Robert's encounters and escapes from the Germans, there was really never any doubt as to his allegiance to the Allies. He was soon allowed to roam free but stayed in one of the SOE's safe houses in the West End. It was a long time since he had been in the UK, racing at Brooklands. All he could think of was getting back to France, to find out what had happened to his parents, his wife and friends. What had happened to Willy Grover? He was unable to bear the thought of Paris being occupied by the Nazis.

His debriefing started two weeks after his return and the SOE decided he was exactly the right sort of chap to be in France helping with their work. They would train him properly over a few months while the search for him in France settled down. Then he would be sent back to continue Willy Grover's work. So he began a three week course in explosives at 17, Brickendonbury under George Rheam's instruction. He was sent on many refresher courses and was given a commission as a Second Lieutenant on the General List of the British Army. He thereafter only appeared as a British officer on the secret War Office lists.

Robert was sent back to France to work around the port of Nantes on the mouth of the River Loire. His code name was Lionel and he was given the alias of Roger Bremontier. This meant that all his initialled belongings could still be used. He was to pick up on Willy's work, whose organisation was now to be called Clergyman.

Clergyman was to consist of four completely separate cells, each with its own targets. One was to be used as a reception committee for arms and explosives, one to target railway lines and links, one to go for electrical substations and pylons lines, putting them out of action for at least a week on D-Day. The final aim was to devise ways of stopping the Germans from destroying the Port of Nantes.

Robert was given half a million francs and told to contact nobody from the old network around that area. His mission was to last around two months; he would be getting out during the January moon without a wireless operator. He was to contact a well proven wireless man called Hercule who was operating from and around Le Mans. Hercule had been a professional radio operator in the 1930s but in 1940, when he was given an English radio set to use, he found it difficult, so he was flown to England and trained by the SOE. While away, his wife and daughter had been arrested by the SD. He was regarded so highly by the SOE he was given free rein to work for any SOE organisation and as many as he liked. He worked for at least six different networks and sent one hundred and thirty eight messages. His secret was never to stay in one place more than one night; he was always on the move. The Germans struggled to keep up with him.

Robert had got near to Paris and found out what had happened to his network. While hiding there he caught up with L'Antoine, his old mechanic, who checked that his Citroën truck was still available. During this time it came to light that Robert's brother, Maurice had got into bed with the Germans and was passing information on. This was confirmed when Maurice was witnessed at the arrest of two other agents. Robert wrote anonymously to as many people he could to advise they could not trust his brother. L'Antoine and Robert then set off for Nantes with all the equipment they could recover from old hiding places.

On route RN10 they tried to avoid checkpoints by taking back roads. They were stopped by a German military policeman and advised they had too many gas cylinders in the vehicle; they must take the policeman into the city and have the vehicle checked over. They knew this was bad news and Robert offered to sit in the back of the truck as it had only two seats in the front. While travelling, Robert lifted as much equipment out as possible and jumped with it. Then he made his way back to Paris. During this trip his suitcase with all his clothes and ID papers sewn into the lining were destroyed. The SD were handed what was left and so had Robert's new ID as well as knowing he had been back in Paris. They quickly brought his brother Maurice in to identify what was left of Robert's clothing to confirm this.

In the meantime L'Antoine had arrived at the police headquarters on Place des Épars in Chartres and was told to unload the truck. He knew this meant arrest and claimed Robert had been a hitch hiker, and that he did not know him. As he unloaded, he waited until the guards got caught up in their own conversation then made a run for it through the narrow streets. The guards chased, firing shots off where they could. Eventually, with no energy left he dived into a florist's; they hid him immediately and he escaped capture. Later he realised how lucky he had been as he found a bullet hole through the bottom of his trousers.

Now Robert had lost his kit he stole a bicycle and rode twenty or so kilometers away from Paris while he reassessed the situation. When he had lost his clothing he had also lost the wireless transmitter, frequency crystals and all the false German blank passes.

He rented a flat in Paris and went under the name of Daniel Perdrige. The real Daniel Perdrige was a member of the Communist Party and had been arrested in 1941 for inciting resistance. He was one of the ninety nine hostages executed at the fort du Mont-Valerien in Suresnes in December 1941. This was a reprisal for the killing of one German officer. Sadly Perdrige left two little girls.

Daniel had a sister who had worked with Robert as part of Chestnut; her code name was Sonia. Robert stayed with her for a short time, realising he had no way of contacting Hercule, as the barman he had to go to make contact - the owner - had been arrested. He went to the Ping Pong bar to find that Henri Dericourt was in the south for another few months. He had no way to communicate with, or return to, England. He decided to make his way to Nantes under his own steam.

Nantes was hit hard because of its strategic value as a port and because it had the first bridge over the Loire. The Allies carried out two massive bombing raids within a week of each other; the first killed fourteen hundred people and destroyed seven hundred buildings plus much other damage. In the second, eight hundred buildings were destroyed and two hundred people were killed. After the second raid, the fire following burned for three days.

Robert returned to Paris and on December 1st, 1944 met Yvonne Grover-Williams and Mme Fremont at the Brasserie Sherry at the Rond-Point des Champs-Elysées. They had arranged to meet with Stella. They discussed Maurice, his brother, as a traitor. They also discussed Willy, as he was being held back in Fresnes. A Swiss delegation had gained the release of one man who had been held there for four months. He had told Mme Fremont that Willy never talked but Maurice wandered around and was never stopped.

Robert went again back to Nantes and started to set up his networks. He soon realised that even with men, without the explosives they could not do their job. He then recruited an ex-Algerian boxer called Petrouche and they started to work from a different angle: to assassinate proven collaborators, to gather information about the SD and make the Germans aware they were now under pressure.

They targeted Karl Bömelberg, the head of the Gestapo in France, who operated from Avenue Foch. The SD Chief Joseph Kieffer, who they knew had interrogated Willy, lived at Avenue Foch just below the prisoners on the fourth floor. They also listed Henri Lafont, a known criminal whose gang worked for the SS from a house on Rue Lauriston.

Robert returned to England and demanded silenced pistols, machine guns, incendiaries devices, grenades and knives. This was granted and on his return Partouche proved to be an exceptional ally; he was able to find out, by masquerading as a sympathiser, where and when the Germans were going to carry out ‘on spec’ raids. They would round up forty to fifty people and check their papers. It was done in the hope that they might flush out collaborators and SOE agents. For Robert this was ideal; he would pass the information on to his men and attack from a base of strength.

Once again he returned to England and was allowed to come back to France. As D-Day was coming closer, he was sent to Nantes with the same objectives plus telecommunication objectives to attack. He was given several code phrases to memorise that would be broadcast by the BBC, warning him when D-Day was imminent, what to attack and when, with all the Resistance men he was able to muster. Once this was organised he would be free to go back to Paris to continue his activities there. He was given his own wireless operator, Denise Bloch, a Jewish athletic girl who had evaded capture once or twice and been an operator since 1942.

This time Robert made sure his brother did not know he was back in Paris.

It was around now that Robert decided to approach Jean-Pierre Wimille. Willy Grover-Williams had not allowed this earlier, but times had changed. Even though Wimille was thirteen years his junior, they had been race partners and really team drivers for Bugatti. They won at Pau and the Le Mans 24 Hours before Wimille had a road accident. He came back later that season and on a skiing trip met his future wife, 'Cric'. A beautiful, slender lady with dark hair who fought alongside

Jean-Pierre for the Resistance, she only just escaped being sent to a concentration camp in Germany in August, 1944. Jean-Pierre was a qualified pilot and was conscripted to fighter training school at Étampes, but after the German invasion he was able to demobilise and then married Cric. He tried to get the Vichy government to support a racing trip to the Indianapolis meeting in the USA. This was denied and he and Cric sold their estate and moved closer to Paris. Wimille, with the help of an ex-Bugatti engineer, started to design post-war production cars. After Willy Grover's arrest, Robert recruited Wimille into his network under the code name of Giles.

On the evening of June 5th, Robert Benoist heard the messages from the BBC he had so long been waiting for and he put his teams into action around Nantes. That night, out of a thousand and fifty raids he had planned and acquired arms for, nine hundred and fifty were completed. His groups halted the movement of all German troops and vehicles in the area of the Dourdan-Rambouillet for quite a while.

Robert Benoist, with as many as he could muster, then returned to Paris, where the Germans were making as many arrests as possible. Robert's group created as much confusion as they could. Robert's mother was very frail after being released from four months' captivity in Fresnes. She died at sixty eight and Robert tried to go and see her. He was unable to get there in time but witnessed the funeral from a distance.

He needed to stay in a safe house that was close because of the curfew, but when he arrived, there were four SS officers waiting for him. He was unarmed and helpless. The SS men called Avenue Foch to let them know they had Benoist and then waited for instructions.

Early in the morning they took Benoist to the SD headquarters, straight to the fifth floor for questioning. He did not give any information away, even though methods of questioning had relaxed since the time of Willy Grover's ordeal. Over a period of a few days eighty percent of Benoist SOE agents were captured. Some of these were able to talk their way out of custody and some were not. Wimille tried to put the operation back together but failed, to a degree.

It was August 24th and the Allies were well on their way to Paris. Vogt invited Benoist's brother to visit Avenue Foch and bring Robert a change of clothes. Benoist asked his brother to pay his rent on the flat and used the opportunity to tell the maid, Chiquita, that he believed he had been given away by an English woman, Violette Szabo. This was never confirmed to me. Maurice informed his brother that he was being deported to Germany the next day!

I cried as Christophe delivered all this overwhelming information. We had obviously missed the chance of helping at Avenue Foch. I let him carry on, as there was obviously more to tell us!

As he told us what was going on and brought us up to date, I noticed that he himself was in terrible shape. He pulled away from any candlelight that was offered up to him, even in the darkness of the catacombs. As my eyes grew more accustomed to the dim light, I began to see why: his skin was white and waxy. A slightly putrid odour seemed to follow him and he shook all the time as if he were cold. He looked damp, if that is possible. Then I noticed he had no eyelids; he could not blink even if he tried. He hid his eyes from the light by bobbing his head forward and allowing his flat cap to protect his eyes, until they became accustomed to the light in front of him.

He had no hair on his face or head that I could be see; just burns and scars. These were nothing like what I had seen before. Glancing down, I could make out he had no fingernails as he scrabbled his fingers on the floor to retrieve a piece of paper he had dropped. Even though there was room to stand in the cavernous part of the catacombs we were in, he did not do so. His ankles were twisted where he had been hobbled. He had not been born like this; it had been done to him.

As Christophe moved, there was a rolling motion to his crawling. Wherever we got to, there would be a bench set up that he could rest at with a low table he could lean on. I could not imagine what he must have been through and as a few tears started to roll down my face, he held out a hand. Using the back of his forefinger he gently and lovingly lifted the tear from my face and smiled at me, revealing a black hole with no teeth.

I shut my eyes and asked, "Who and When?"

He replied, "I worked with Willy Grover; I was one of his mechanics. Do you not remember me? We have met many times before. When you were a little girl you came around the garage on my shoulders as we followed Will and Robert round the workshop, looking to improve the cars while discussing ideas for modifications and improvements. When they taught you to drive, I was always there with the starting handle to spin your Austin's engine over after you stalled it. If it broke, I fixed it for you. Can you not remember 'Christophe le Grand'? At this moment I remembered who he was and my emotions began to well up inside me.

He carried on talking. "The Boch never knew Mr. Grover and I had a connection. They knew I was with the Resistance but had no idea how close he and I had worked together. The day Willy was taken away to Berlin, I was dropped off at hospital to recover again from my treatment at the hands of the kind and well-meaning Miss

Ranndue. It was from the hospital I was brought here, by a few very special and brave nurses Anna and Rachael, with doctors Thomas and John. I never saw those caring people again, but for a while medication seemed to appear while I was able to sleep. Maybe they were caught or moved - I have no idea.

'Since then the catacombs have become my home. I help the Resistance where I can and gather data for the Allies when they arrive. When this is all over I hope to organise a new form of resistance: the type all will cheer for, even though they will know nothing of who we are. The authorities will have to turn a blind eye to our activities – our aim is to repair the things that are broken in this the great city of Paris. We will repair the clocks in the towers that do not work. We will take away the broken things high up, that people never see, and return them in perfect order. My volunteer army of artisans will be unknown and unseen like myself!

"Sorry, I digress, sweetheart," said

Christophe, as he spat on the ground while his eyes watered and glazed over. "Miss Ranndue works for Vogt. She is particularly vicious and where he found that one metre, thirty five centimetre piece of Hell I will never know. When you think it is over and you want to give up and die, she sits and waits like a praying mantis. You dare not move or show signs of life as she watches from somewhere. Arriving in her pristine laundered civilian clothes, she smiles at you. Her little pointy ears and pixie eyebrows disguise the hell she has been dreaming up for you that day. Petite and slim, with those blue eyes and mouse-coloured hair, she gives nothing away of the anger and pain that must be inside her. I think she never treats the women prisoners with her particular kind of love. Little games such as matches under your fingernails being lit are such soft, lovers' things to do.

'She will drill through a man's fingernails one at a time, as his wrists are tied down so the hand and fingers are immobilised. This is done one at a time - maybe two fingers or toes a day. With clay, a little funnel will then be placed and moulded over the drill hole, just as you would do to put acid into a lock, or to shape explosives. Then slowly an acid will be placed into the clay funnel. This will start to tickle for maybe two or three seconds. I think it must have been sulphuric acid as it was quite thick. It seemed to hunt water.

'Once it was through the unbroken skin under the drilled nail it went wild. The pain was so intense I fainted several times, only to wake up in a cell with a clean, throbbing undressed wound. These were so tender; a breath of air sent me into agonising pain. You remember my height and my hair? The scalp was burnt with an acetylene torch and my ankles broken so many times I cannot remember. A bag over the head, your head held back and water thrown over it continuously so you can not breathe is child's play. I know she worked at a concentration camp and loved to tap away at Jewish captives' privates with a pencil; tapping away for an amount of time, so that over a day or two their testis turned black. This was just repeated every day for no reason other than her pleasure of hurting men.

'God, what is in her mind I do not know! Since the Allies landed she has travelled north, I think to Holland. It could be Amsterdam, Rotterdam or Utrecht; she could be anywhere with another sneaky sick bastard! I am sure this will be to hide, and come the end of the war play the innocent! If you see her, do not be taken in by the smile and the gestures. Be warned, you will be dispatched without a thought entering her head, just as a mouse in a trap. Thoughtless, deadly and with intent! I pray she does not team up with others with such malice within them selves."

I grimaced, as did Albert, Erich and Stuart as the realisation of the terror in Christophe's eyes unveiled the rest of the truth. My stomach had churned to see that this gentle man had been mutilated into such a physical mess. He obviously still had the heart of a lion as he had mentioned and planned for the future. There was nothing we could do to help him, but maybe we could still help Uncle Willy and Uncle Robert. If anyone had an idea of what was going on and where, Christophe did!

He went on to let us know the following: as the Allied troops were battling their way out of Normandy, the number of executions was sadly increasing day by day. We were told that Robert had been sent to Fresnes, where nearly three thousand prisoners were being held. This was nearly half the total number of prisoners being held in the whole of Paris. The prison was badly overcrowded and the prisoners were very jumpy.

Each morning the prisoners waited to find out who would be facing a firing squad. They found out by listening to the iron-wheeled carts as they delivered coffee (acorn) to the inmates in cells along the corridors. If the cart passed a cell, the prisoners within knew they were staying. If the cart stopped at a cell, the prisoners would then be informed who was to be executed, and who was to be deported.

That was August 8th and Uncle Robert was now being deported with a very special group of prisoners. I urged Christophe to hurry as it was now August 9th; we had no time to plan, but maybe we could do something.

The prisoners had been assembled onto three prison buses. The first two were for males and the last for females. They were nearly all SOE agents from all around France. I do not know how many Robert knew. They had quietly glanced and acknowledged each other, but nobody spoke, as nobody knew who might be an infiltrator and who were using what aliases. It would be safer to acknowledge a friend at a better time. Before they boarded the buses, the prisoners were handcuffed into pairs and handed an International Red Cross food parcel. This I can only assume gave a little hope and encouragement. The buses departed and quickly drove through Paris to Gare de l'Est, where the Germans were putting a train together to run across northeastern France to Germany.

The train had left that day and we raced to find a way to follow; Christophe got us out of Paris by routes none of us would ever have found or could remember. Sadly I never saw him again. I hope Christophe survived; he did more for us in a few hours than I can ever remember or could have thanked him for.

Once we got out of Paris to the east, we were able to pick up the railway line that Christophe had suggested would be the most likely route. He had drawn a map that was pretty accurate. He had also suggested a few farmers who might be able to help us with horses, as well as velos (a small, two-stroke pedalled motorbike) that we could borrow to travel quickly on less well checkpointed roads. He supplied us with a map or two, the all important timepiece and compass and the whereabouts of checkpoints and fuel depots for vehicles.

It took us a day to get ahead of the train using every bit of guile we could muster. The train was a converted troop carrier and was to return injured soldiers from the retreating front. By this time the Allies had almost complete control of the air and so the Germans had painted red crosses on the trains. The American P-47 Thunderbolt fighter-bomber pilots were aware of this and would attack anyway. The last carriage on this train had an anti-aircraft gun on it, as many of their trains had been attacked and some destroyed. The prisoner carriage was coupled to the anti-aircraft bogie; it housed several guards as well as the prisoners.

We were later to find that out that the prisoners were housed as follows: nine handcuffed pairs into one compartment, eight handcuffed pairs into another and three female prisoners into another part with the guards. There was no ventilation and all the windows had been knocked out and then boarded over. In the carriage were probably the SD's most wanted men and women.

These included Stephane Hessel, one of General de Gaulle's secret agents; Yeo-Thomas, Major Henri Frager and Squadron Leader Maurice Southgate, a legend in the southwest of France. About half of the prisoners were French; the rest were Belgian, British or American. There were others from networks such as Major Henry Fraser, François Garel, Emile Henri Garry, Pierre Culioli and a couple of Canadians, Captain John McAlister and Captain Frank Pickersgill, who was in a very bad physical state. He had been wounded four times while trying to escape from a German prison in Paris. He had attacked a guard with a broken bottle and jumped from a second floor window. While running, he was hit four times by machine gun fire. Also in the carriage were Harry Peuleve and Philippe Liewer, whom Benoist had met in London; Lieutenants Marcel Leccia, Elisée Allard, Pierre Geelen, Captain Pierre Mulsant, Flying Officer Dennis Barret and Captain Gerald Keun. Benoist was handcuffed to the American George Wilkinson who had been parachuted into France in May, 1944 - weeks before D-Day. Hessel survived the war and later he was to say that the guards kept moving up and down the trucks to make sure none of the prisoners were up to any tricks. Otherwise they were left alone in the heat and stench.

While we were getting ahead of the train, more and more ambulances had been arriving and delivering injured soldiers. They had not been in a hurry to leave the station until dusk fell, in the hope that the dark would protect them. Finally the train had pulled out of Gare de l'Est; it worked its way out of the city through Pantin, Noisy, Bondy and Raincy to reach the river Marne. It headed out over the old World War One battlefields. It was impossible for the prisoners to rest, with the train continuously stopping and starting. Yves Loison tried endlessly to pick the lock on his handcuffs and the only discussion was if Loison managed to do it, should they make a run for it.

By dawn the train had not even got as far as

Épernay in the Champagne hills. The heat and no water made it very difficult, and the guards were getting more and more on edge as they approached the flat land towards Chalons-sur-Marne (Now Chalons-en-Champagne).

That day, an air raid had been planned on the Mercedes Benz factory at Sindelfingen, near Stuttgart amongst others. The US Eighth Air Force heading for the targets hit bad weather and many had to turn back with their fighter escorts. In addition there were more than one hundred P47s escorted by P51 Mustangs attacking communication targets, wherever they found them.

That afternoon some P47s spotted the train and attacked. The train came to a sudden stop. The prisoners knew the train was under attack and could hear the anti-aircraft firing with committed enthusiasm. The guards ran and during this period the prisoners were able to get water from the lavatory into a container and get it passed round to each other.

Once the raid was over, the guards took their time to return. The train was too damaged to continue and once the Germans had dealt with their own injured, they turned up with two trucks, loading the prisoners onto them. This was thirty hours after they had departed. We were so close to them - if it had not been for the air raid we probably would not have caught up. From a distance we saw the trucks leave with our objective. They were taken to Gestapo headquarters in the centre of Chalons. We got into Chalons just after they had left; we were told that in the confusion of the guards trying to get orders, the prisoners had been allowed to at least wash in the town centre fountain. A few of the prisoners had been able to briefly talk with locals and had given messages in the hope they would get some information to their families.

They were following Route Nationale 3 to Verdun. We followed and travelled overnight to witness them leaving Verdun in the morning, heading towards the German border. We had to rest, knowing that potentially we had missed another opportunity to free them. There was just never any time to re-group our thoughts, find some weapons or create a plan. We just had to follow again without being discovered. As we headed through Metz, people were beginning to realise the war was almost over and were showing greater signs of hostility to the Germans. This gave us hope and we started to acquire help. This was in the form of small arms, directions and horses so we could travel cross-country.

We crossed the border, now even more wary and found the prison camp they had been taken to. KZ Neue Bremm was situated close to Saarbrücken; it was an SS run transit camp. It was an evil looking place, the like I had never imagined could exist. We found a vantage point and dug in. We were all in awe of the watchtowers – nine foot high fences topped with electrified barbed wire.

The women had been separated off and taken to another camp. I believe they were taken to Ravensbrück in the forests north of Berlin.

As the men were unloaded into the camp, they were beaten and kicked by the SS guards. I think they were shocked and distraught. Looking through my binoculars I was crying. How the hell were we going to be able to effect a rescue now? This was a real concentration camp; we were able to see the prisoners now being chained by the ankle to each other in groups of five and six. To go to the latrine they shuffled along and if one of them stumbled the SS guards immediately beat them. It was unbelievably vicious.

The special prisoners, my men, were chained in pairs and were taken to a hut behind the kitchen not more than ten by ten feet. It had one tiny window and we were able to see nothing. It must have been hell: mid-summer, hot, no room and no ventilation. Occasionally they were brought out, only to witness beatings and then put back in.

After three days, we still had no plan. We were still in a daze and shocked that this could be going on! The prisoners were brought out, loaded onto trucks again and taken to Saarbrücken station and I thought we had lost them. Erich stepped in and with his ability to speak German got us more information. This train was going to the city of Weimar and that would take less than one day. We pushed on as hard as would could; it took us three days. God knows what had been happening to our boys. We followed the railway lines looking for sidings, run-offs and spurs that would seem not to have heavy traffic. One led us north of the city and we could see special fences around the end of this spur line. The camp was called KZ Buchenwald. It was here that medical experiments were being held on human beings.

When we arrived and found a safe place to dig in, we saw a group of prisoners arrive. I could only presume Uncle Robert was in there. The prisoners of war were stripped and shaved in the open, sprayed with chemicals then dipped like sheep. We could smell how strong the stuff was from three quarters of a mile away. There were thirteen guard towers with nine foot fences, topped with electrified barbed wire again.

The prisoners wore uniforms that we could see were differentiated by two markings - a red triangle, which we later found out was for political prisoners, and yellow for Jewish. All were slave laboured for next to no rations. There were strange buildings producing a lot of smoke, which we assumed were some sort of power producing station, but there were no power lines leaving the camp and no fuel dumps. We had heard stories, but this could not be what we were witnessing.

In the end we did find out exactly what happened. Out of all the chaps we had chased in the hope of at least freeing Uncle Robert, three survived. This was due to a sympathetic doctor and some very brave Jews. The rest fell to Hitler's Special Orders: no SOE agents were to survive the war. They were to be given 'special treatment'; this meant to be hung by piano wire or taken to the crematorium, gassed below it and then burned. No paper trail or evidence of his or her existence was to remain. We counted them in and never got the opportunity to count them out again.

At this point I was past most forms of reason, and even when the Americans came through, the four of us remained in hiding. For me, life was over. Everything I cared about was lost or so damaged it could never be revived. Erich and Stuart had a long, hard talk with me as we slowly made our way back towards Montreux.

Erich talked to me and said, "If I led them, they would work with me, not to avenge what we have witnessed, but to help real people wherever we can and if necessary or required, stop any organisation or tyrant doing what Hitler and the Nazis have tried to do. In other words FIGHT FOR LIBERTY!"

This came about in the following way: as we

made our way back to Switzerland, we witnessed several persons acting in - well, not a suspicious or out of the ordinary way! They just stood out slightly. Was it was because they had been too well fed, or their mannerisms were too overpowering to others? It may just have been confidence - having too much. Then it dawned on us one at a time: these were bloody German SS men, on the run to Switzerland to hide. Well I can tell you now; they were not going to get past us.

Once we worked out how to spot them, they became really quite easy to see. I know that much later, when searches were going on in the fifties and sixties, they had much trouble in finding them. Time changes people, as does the environment they are in. For us it was not so bad; they could disguise themselves all they wanted, but they could not hide several things when on the road. Arrogance always shows through even in the defeated, yet these monsters thought they were going to get away with their actions as well as the goods stolen from prisoners. They carried too much weight, walked too loosely and without pain. Their skin was full and not gaunt. Generally they were cleaner and did not stink like those who had not bathed for months. They would always skulk away from uniformed Allied personnel and troops. When they saw any Allied personnel headed for them, any refugee I had seen looked for news of what was happening and for food and anything they maybe were able to offer. These German SS guys did exactly the opposite. Some would try and look like this but no, it was too demeaning for the nasty little men.

So we started to watch from a distance, not too far from Strasburg, in France - a main thoroughfare for people to enter Switzerland, but not from Germany. Obviously the ones who had got this far must speak pretty good French, as well as their native tongue. We were not cut-throats, but were interested to see what they carried with them. They seemed to always be well provisioned and able to buy whatever they wanted. We were living off the land with very little and they looked pretty well fed, so it was time to have a good look at a few.

The first one we took to one side played all the usual games. This is an outrage etc. Once he realised we were acting on our own, things started to change a little. There would be no trial, no Geneva Convention to rely on and lets face it - we had seen enough of their methods. One of the early ones we caught, Stuart recognised as one of the German SS officers from the last camp we had been watching. He quickly admitted he had been an officer there but was only following orders. He thought he had been lucky to escape before the Americans had arrived. He thought wrong!

I still had not calmed down and took it out on him. There was not much left of him by the time I had finished. He was never going to feel fresh air inflate his lungs again. However we did learn the following: part of the jewellery taken from prisoners' belongings and teeth etc. had remained on campus by order of the commandant. When the SS camp staff etc. went on the run, they had split it between each other to help get a new start in life wherever they were running to. We had no idea how many of these men were doing this and from how many camps. What I did know was that we could catch a lot of them – those who would otherwise slip through the net. We could humiliate them and then decide what to do with the acquired gold and jewellery. The boys agreed it could do no harm and if it was therapeutic for me, so much the better.

We followed a pretty simple method of operation: if you looked too good, then you probably were. We only went for individuals and pairs, just in case they were armed. We did probably let a few through the net if we were not absolutely convinced of their former employer. However, when we were convinced it went as follows: we would take them away from the road and into the local hills for a little chat. We stripped them naked - if it was raining, all the better. We would then go through their belongings - bags, suitcases - you name it, we destroyed it. Then we would go through all their clothing and destroy that. We did find, while we were doing this, diamonds, gold, gem stones and silver.

We would then hold these prisoners for the few days that we worked the area. Then as we moved on, to avoid difficulties with the authorities we would leave them in groups tied up with no clothes. We would leave notes around them explaining that they were ex-SS troops or officers and that freedom fighters for the Resistance had secured them. I don't think we were ever going to be chased down for these thefts, but it was better to try and leave it as clean as possible.

We carried on doing this for quite a while, then headed towards Dole as the amount of stuff we had acquired was becoming alarmingly large. It took us eight days to get to Charles with our load.

He happily put us up in our usual hideout while we decided what to do next.

The result was to smelt everything down and separate it all out into small manageable amounts. Each amount was to be just about enough for a person who was frugal to get a start in life.

We then went out distributing these packages to refugees who we could be pretty certain were genuine. I do still hope that these persons actually did get another chance in life, and were able to dismiss the horrors from their minds.

I have always tried to be the best of the best, fair and straight at all times. You will be the judge of that as you receive subsequent diaries from Ron Kirk.

Entry 9: Return to Racing

On May 29th, 1945 the bells rang out at Saint Pierre church in Neuilly-sur-Seine. The memorial service was for Robert Benoist. Many of his racing colleagues were able to attend and obviously some sadly were not. They were there to honour the sacrifice Robert had made for a free world. There was even a discrete wreath from the British Embassy and a group of people from the Consulate, I was told. For many it was an unpleasant surprise to see Robert's brother, Maurice present. He defended himself enthusiastically against the rumours that he had worked with the Germans, but I do not know as I had not been involved.

Erich and Stuart headed back to Montreux in early August. We all thought we had done enough by then. We had agreed that once my debriefing with Vera Atkins and probably Buckmaster of the SOE was over, I would demobilise myself and find a new carrier. This would safeguard all of us, as I had been 'off-piste' so long I could not know what might happen on my return to the UK. The intention was that Albert would stay in Dole at the monastery with Charles, after he had returned to Elvington in the UK. It meant there was an excuse to thank again W.C. Jack Butler and let him know I had found Albert and we had some ideas for the future.

All of the monies we had not been able to distribute would be held by Charles for use in the future and as a pension. As none of us really knew what the world had in store for us, we agreed to meet again in two years' time at the Monastery with Charles.

Albert and I were in transit through Paris when we heard about the race; we were so excited, we stayed in the hope that I might see old friends. Those who were from the pre-war racing world wanted to honour Uncle Robert, and Maurice Mestivier, president of the Association

General Automobiles des Couriers Independents, began planning a race meeting, to take place as soon as the War was over in Europe. It was decided that a race would be good for morale, especially if it was held in Paris, as thousands of people would be able to attend.

Mestivier had been a mechanic in 1921 for Amilcar and then became a driver himself, later becoming Amilcar's chief engineer. He had worked closely with André Morel and had been in competition with Benoist, selling production road cars before the war. Maurice Mestivier had become president of the AGACI in 1937 and even with the backing of one of the largest Resistance organisations it was still difficult to organise a race so soon after the war. They had agreed that any profit from the race would go to former prisoners of the war and war victims. The main difficulties were not the authorities, but racing cars; there were no new ones - many had been hidden away six years ago and were in a poor state of repair.

Racing tyres were near impossible to find. The easy part was the road circuit itself. This was in the Bois de Boulogne, the woodland park. It is just west of Paris and close to the Metro station Porte Dauphine.

The start-finish line was set close to the boating lake at Carrefour du Bout des Lacs. The pits were on Route de Surenses, running from the crossroads to Port Dauphine. It was only a few hundred yards from Avenue Foch, the old SD headquarters where we had been so close and yet so far away from helping Robert. At Port Dauphine there was a hairpin turn that sent the drivers back into the park, running down Allée des Fortifications along to Avenue de Saint-Cloud and then round to the right until it reached the junction with chemin de Ceinture du Lac Inférieur. This hairpin sent them back towards the pits through an extremely technical part of the track for the drivers. The six hundred yards here went through two sets of S-bends with the boating lake on their left hand side.

Then they arrived back at Carrefour du Bout des Lacs, which now had become a very high-speed right hand corner. What a cracking track - just under two miles.

Preparations for the race had gone on through the summer. The war in the Pacific was going in the direction the Allies expected and was coming to an end slowly. The Americans dropped the second atomic bomb in August and the Japanese surrendered. Two weeks later, the official documents were signed on USS Missouri in Tokyo Bay.

Seven days after that, between ninety and two hundred thousand spectators turned out to see the first motor race since the end of World War Two. We were there Nick! We were there!

It was named the 'Coupe Robert Benoist', a thirty six lap race for cars of 750cc to 1.5 litres. Seventeen had entered, including three tuned and prepped by Amédée Gordini for Jean Brault, Robert Cayeux and for himself. Two old Salmsons were entered for Just-Émile Vernet and Robert-Aimé Bouchard, and a pair of Rileys driven by the engineer Pierre Ferrand and Georges Brunot. Charles Deutsch, the engineer, had designed and was to drive his DB. A Singer was entered by Jacques Savoye. Victor Polledry entered and drove an Aston Martin, while the rest of the field was made up of an Alder, an Amilcar, Fiat and one small Bugatti. I only knew a few of the drivers, but I knew only too well the smell of burning racing oil, and the musical notes being blown out of the cars' exhausts.

Just before the first race, Ettore Bugatti rolled up in a Bugatti Royale and the crowd rushed forward. With the help of the US military police and the police of Paris, they were just able to contain the crowd.

In the thirty six lap race, Gordini took the lead on lap one and continued to lead his teammates through the whole sixty two mile race. Nobody seemed to care about the result - they loved the sound and excitement of the race.

Then all fell silent. A lone bugle sounded out the 'Last Post' as the crowd stood for a minute's silence in memory of Robert Benoist. He had done so much for French motor racing, even more for France and again for liberty. His daughter, Jacqueline Garnier, was presented with a bouquet of flowers. We sat with her before the second race and cried at our loss of these especially brave gladiators of the track.

Once the tribute was over and emotions had settled down, the engines of the competitors' cars for the main race began to roar into life. The race had been named 'Coupe de la Liberation'. It was for engines from 1.5 litres to 3 litres in capacity. Out of the fifteen entrants there were six Amilcars, one of these driven by Mestivier. René Bonnet, a co-founder of DB, was in one of his own cars. Auguste Veuillet drove an MG (he had been a motorcycle racer and later became Porsche's importer of cars to France). Polledry appeared in an

Alfa Romeo 1750. This race was won by Henri Louveau, with ease in a Maserati 6CM - his was the only 3 litre car entered. We walked through the pits and I introduced Albert to the drivers I knew from the old days. It was so good to be in the environment I so much enjoyed.

Thanks to the intervention of a friend, Jean-Pierre Wimille and Captain François Sommer (Raumond's brother) had arranged for a release from duty fighting against some German stronghold. Wimille arrived too late to take part in the practice or qualifying and was told he would have to start from the back of the grid. When I saw him I ran towards him, Berty in hot pursuit, not knowing where I was going. When Jean-Pierre spotted me, he dropped to his knees to catch me and we both cried. At least one of my great heroes had survived. Berty and I had prepped the great Bugatti as best we could, knowing a driver was coming, but I had no idea it was to be my friend.

For me the prepping was fun and I think

Berty enjoyed it too. It was great not to be in a life and death struggle and under that crazy pressure. So we had fun doing it, washing and polishing right through from stem to stern. We had an advantage though, as Uncle Robert, in typical style, had already arranged most things for us: there was new oil and new filters for us; new spark plugs; new points, high tension leads and distributor cap. In fact the only things we didn't replace but cleaned and adjusted were the brake shoes, as new ones would need bedding in. We emptied the fuel tank and blew her lines out, cleaned the carburettors out and made sure the advance and retard for the ignition was working correctly. There were new tyres to put on and so on. I knew it would be the most reliable and best prepared car there. We ran the engine up to temperature several times and took her for a little spin. Boy, she was a monster and so damned fast! I could even hold a powerslide in her with ease - a little oversteer and and a tiny excess throttle - just a dream.

After the great fuss, I filled him in on what had happened to his driving partners. We cried again and drank a toast to them. Jean-Pierre then introduced himself to Berty and told us what he could of his war. We agreed that he must win the big race in Uncle Robert's Bugatti. Jean-Pierre agreed and swore on his life, he would! I had walked the track with Albert early that morning so I went through the racing lines with him, then drew out on the ground where the track was in bad condition, as it could cause tyre failure, or a reduction in adhesion to the surface, resulting in a lack of acceleration or requiring earlier deceleration. He took it all in hand and thanked me, as he had had no opportunity to get round the track. I must say he was fired up and ready to go.

Uncle Robert had hidden away his factory type 59/50B Bugatti works car that had been hidden in 1939 before the Germans could steal it. It had an eight-cylinder engine, producing 450 horsepower and Jean-Pierre was going to drive it!

Sommer had qualified at the front in his Talbot - he would probably be Jean-Pierre's biggest rival - but his Talbot only produced 250 horses.

The main event had sixteen entrants. Their cars were over 3 litres and the winning prize was for the trophy 'Coupe des Prisonniers'. Seven of the entrants were driving Delahaye 135Ss. The drivers included Eugene Carboud, winner of the 1938 Le Mans 24 hours. The cars were pretty much out of date but most of the big name drivers of the 1930s were present. Philippe Étancelin, at forty nine years old, was probably past his best; he was driving an Alfa Romeo 8C. Louis Gerard was driving a ten year old Maserati 8CM. Raymond Sommer had a T26 Talbot, Lago and Pierre Levegh a Talbot 150C.

There were five Bugattis: the T55 driven by Paul Friderich, the son of Ernest the Bugatti dealer from Nice. Maurice Trintignant was twenty eight and hoping to make a name for himself in racing in a Type 35/51, which he called 'Grandma' - it dated back to the early 1930s. His brother, Louis Trintignant, had originally raced it and was killed in it at the Grand Prix of Picardie during practice. At that time Maurice was sixteen and the family had sold the car. He had bought it back five years later and had just started racing it as the war broke out. He had been doing really well and was the protégé of Jean-Pierre Wimille, who was becoming the big Bugatti star of the time. During the war 'Grandma' had been hidden under a haystack in a barn in the area of Vaucluse. As soon as the war had come to an end, he had started to restore her.

Jean-Pierre was the biggest star of the Coupe des Prisonniers. He told me that after he had escaped a raid on his SOE cell at Sermaise, he had fought with the surviving members of the Turma Vengeance movement in the Dourdan area. As Paris was liberated, he liaised between the Allied forces and the Resistance. Once that had all settled down he enlisted with the Forces Aériennes Françaises Libres. After his training he joined

Groupe de Reconnaissance 111/33, based in Cognac, flying Bell P-63s on missions against a heavy pocket of German resistance around Royan.

The state of preparation was fairly poor and out of sixteen entrants, nine failed to finish the Coupe des Prisonniers. But as the flag dropped and the cars roared away, the crowd was on its feet. Jean-Pierre Wimille was ninth by the first corner. Seesawing at the wheel like a possessed hero, he was fourth by the end of the first lap. He then pushed his way past the man in second place, sliding out of the big right-hander at the start–finish line. He then settled and set about chasing the leader, Sommer. The ground shook under the big Bugatti as it braked hard, and then stilled as we were deafened by the ear-drumming sound of the straight-through exhaust of the big eight cylinder engine. My knees shook with pleasure on hearing such music. The smell of the roaring engine, the pale blue smoke puffing out of the exhaust when the throttles were closed on the overrun, was just like being in heaven.

It took a few laps to catch Sommer in the Talbot, setting his car up into bends slightly sideways to get the best drive out of the corners. When he did catch him they were entering the double set of S-bends and Sommer deliberately balked Jean-Pierre. This caused Jean-Pierre to allow a slightly larger gap to develop through the bends and Sommer was able to hold him through the rest of the lap. The next time round, Jean-Pierre had Sommer set up with a feint to the right and what looked like an outbraking attempt in the big Bugatti. What he really did was get Sommer in the Talbot to come slightly off-line on his entry into the double S-bends. That was all Jean-Pierre needed; he stuck close to the Talbot all the way through. As they exited the S-bends, Sommer kept a tight line round the long right-hander, coming onto the start-finish straight. The Bugatti, sticking tight to the Talbot's tail, started to drift out wider and wider as it drifted under the enormous torque of the engine.

Then Jean-Pierre went up another gear and the race was over - his Bugatti pulled away and left the Talbot like a floundering fish. They were not even in the same race any more; the Bugatti and Jean-Pierre just kept pulling away until the flag was dropped.

After the race, Jean-Pierre Wimille told reporters, “The car was extraordinary! With this car I can win other races.”

On the rostrum, Jean-Pierre received the Coupe des Prisonniers trophy and the crowd cheered and started to celebrate. They then all fell silent as a very frail old man with shaven head worked his way to the rostrum with the help of some stewards. He had with him a trophy. His name was Albert Fremont, and he was one of the few survivors of the Buchenwald concentration camp. He was there to present the winner of the Coupe des Prisonniers with the trophy Coupe Williams. The cup had been donated by Jean Boudon, an old friend of Willy and Yvonne Grover.

It was presented in Uncle Willy's honour to Jean-Pierre Wimille.

After a few days, when the excitement had died down, Albert and I headed back to the UK. My debriefing took longer than I thought and at the end I was asked to take a job in the civilian sector. This was to be under a chap called Ian Fleming, who had been in Navy Intelligence during the war, but now was to be running a group of reporters through the Times Newspaper. At the time I had no real idea of what I was to be doing, although I was advised it was the correct thing to do, as I had all the relevant experience and would probably excel at it.

Chapter 9: Remembrance

Nick sat at his dark oak desk with the green leather inlay, slowly taking in the information given to him by the diary. He felt the odd shiver down his spine as he remembered some of the things they had done together, all those years ago. The way she said 'yheeesss' in that elongated, questioning way - as if you were supposed to already know the answer. They way she drove the Healey; was it wild or was it done with sublime control! Her comments on why it was so uprated for power and control, such as "my employer liked to know I could move if I needed to!"

He remembered her words: "I know a bad one from a good one and I've dispatched a few in my time!" She could shoot, she could poach and she was bright, boy she had been bright. Neat, tidy, clinical and methodical as well as damned good fun to be with. Could this diary be true? He remembered the funeral - all the different nationalities that had shown up and left such similar cards. As he did this, tears slowly ran down his face, dripping onto his desk, just missing the diary.

His daughter of four slowly sidled into Nick's office and stood next to him, her little right foot crossed over her left, arms folded in the style of a ballerina. Little Phillipa had come to see why Daddy had not come to the village event and why he was missing all the fun.

She saw Daddy was crying and asked, as she started to tug at his sleeve, "Daddy why are you sad? Everybody outside is having fun. I've had a go at catch the ferret, the bouncy castle and the Jumpoline – it's great Daddy. Please, please come and be happy with us."

Nick replied, "Oh little Philly I'm so sorry, I know it's a special day! I'll be along in just half an hour. Check your watch mind, and come and get me. I'll be ready then, but for now I just have to look a few things up, so that I can keep a promise."

Little Philly, satisfied with her father's answer, trotted off back to the village event to have as much fun as possible.

Nick carried on pondering what to do next. He thought about all those pictures with the great racing riders and drivers and began to smile while leaning forward to turn his computer on. His smile was raw, almost a grimace. Had he been so naive those few years ago that he had not been listening to Murtyl? Or had he been so preoccupied with life that he had not listened to her? Had she really just at times spoken in such a way that everything would fall into place when he received the diaries? There was obviously a great deal more to find out from subsequent diaries, but for now he had to check out names and dates on his computer through this Internet thing. At least Ron Kirk, the solicitor had been right - now the "World Wide Web" was available, the research would be infinitely easier and faster.

Firstly he checked out "Willy Grover-

Williams" and his racing history, then Mr. Williams' picture against the picture of Mr. Williams and Murtyl together. He smiled now with admiration, while commenting to himself, "I'm beginning to think this all could be true!"

Secondly he looked up Mr. Robert Benoist and his racing history and compared Mr. Benoist's picture with one Nick still had of Murtyl with Mr Benoist. This was a match too!

War records of the above were not available and still classed as secret. He pondered and then looked up Avenue Foch in Paris and found who had been using certain buildings and what for during the war. It checked out! He then looked up the career of Jean-Pierre Wimille as well as the results of the great race held in Paris on September 15th, 1945 and started to jump for joy. As far as he was concerned, he agreed with Murtyl: her story had to be told.

He left his office to walk outside, striding across to the village green. He walked up to one of the great oak trees and placed his palm on it. Looking up to the cloudless sky, he said out loud as a great shiver ran down his spine, “I say it again Murtyl. I now have seen a little of what you have done. I believe in you and will never let you down. Thank you for trusting me; may your God bless you wherever you are.”

Philly turned up at her father’s side and asked in her precocious manner, “Are you finished Daddy?”

“Yheees,” he said in that questioning way.

“Are you coming to play now?”

“Yheees,” he said, while his mind was still wandering.

He was soon brought back to reality by the quick-witted cheeky little Phillipa, as she started to run towards the next stall she wanted to play at. “But your legs aren’t moving!”

Nick sighed, pushed himself away from the tree and gave chase.

END of book one!

Acknowlegements and User References taken from:

The Grand Prix Saboteurs by Joe Saward.

A Life in Secrets by Sarah Helm.

Mrs Mahoney's Secret War by Gretel Mahoney and Claudia Strachan.

The Bugati Queen by Miranda Seymour.

The Heroines of SOE. Britain's Secret Woman in France. F Section.

By Squadron Leader Beryl E. Escott.

Outwitting the Gestapo by Lucie Aubrac.

Moondrop to Gascony by Anne Marie Walters.

ABOUT THE AUTHOR

Dr Chris Pearson is a doctor of traditional medicines who treats private patients, human and equine. He tends to prefer treating equine patients as it is more of a challenge. His inspiration to start the

Murtyl Diaries was through his sporting knowledge of motor cycles and his interest in historic vehicles and racing drivers from the pre World War II years. A time when an Amateur could compete with the Professionals and still prove to be a winner.

DISCLAIMER

All of the characters in this book are fictitious, and any resemblance to actual persons, living or dead, is purely coincidental. Except for those persons of historical significance mentioned within the book's User Reference.

As a first time writer I would like to thank friend, nieghbours and family who have been the inspiration at the beginning and helping through the process of producing my first novel. I am still astounded it has ever happened!

Sarah Harbour.

Brian and Jill Nichols

Lex Ruddiman

Lucinda & Cara Egerton

Hob

Jack

Johny

Jo

Cpt N.Pearson

Kevin

&

Steve Robinson.

95312875R00163

Made in the USA
Columbia, SC
10 May 2018